KU-067-759

STORM-VOICE

JUDY ALLEN

**Hodder
Children's
Books**

a division of Hodder Headline Limited

Laois County Library
Leabharlann _____ Laoise

Acc. No. _____ 06/2034

Class No. _____ JF

Inv. No. _____ 8369

Copyright © 2003 Judy Allen

First published in Great Britain in 2003
by Hodder Children's Books
as part of Hodder Silver Series

The right of Judy Allen to be identified as the Author
of the Work has been asserted by her in accordance with the
Copyright, Designs and Patents Act 1988.

10 9 8 7 6 5 4 3 2 1

All rights reserved. No part of this publication may be
reproduced, stored in a retrieval system, or transmitted,
in any form or by any means without the prior written
permission of the publisher, nor be otherwise circulated
in any form of binding or cover other than that in which
it is published and without a similar condition being
imposed on the subsequent purchaser.

All characters in this publication are fictitious and any resemblance
to real persons, living or dead, is purely coincidental.

A Catalogue record for this book is available from
the British Library

ISBN 0 340 85443 X

Typeset by Avon Dataset Ltd, Bidford-on-Avon, Warks

Printed and bound in Great Britain by
Clays Ltd, St Ives plc

The paper and board used in this paperback by
Hodder Children's Books are natural recyclable products
made from wood grown in sustainable forests. The manufacturing
processes conform to the environmental regulations of
the country of origin.

Hodder Children's Books
a division of Hodder Headline Limited
338 Euston Road
London NW1 3BH

To L. J.

ONE

Like all their kind, the dusty shells, standing in a line on a shelf, held the sounds of the sea.

The sight of them evoked memories, too, but not every memory – only the happy ones, of the child crouching on the beach, stirring through the pebbles, intent on the hunt.

And the sounds they held weren't all the sounds they had heard. The larger shells, the ones big enough to press to the ear and listen to, seemed full of the sigh and rush of the water, the rattling drag as it pulled back through the shingle, the crash of the waves falling on the shore – even the wild roaring and surging of a storm . . .

. . . But not the screaming. Somehow they hadn't recorded the screaming.

TWO

Where does a story begin? Where does this one begin? Does it begin with the screaming, or with the accident, or with that earlier event which – directly or indirectly – caused both?

Or does it begin even further back, when two people met, and married, and had a daughter . . .

Perhaps it begins with something very minor, like a simple refusal to go on holiday.

Katie knew she wasn't taking the refusal well, but she couldn't help it. Every spring half-term and every autumn half-term the two families went away together for a week. They had done this for as long as she could remember.

Sometimes they camped. More often they rented a simple house somewhere. It was always too small, and occasionally something vital broke down – the cooker or the hot water – but none of that ever mattered. They took turns to sleep in beds or on inflatable mattresses on the floor. Often two or three of them had to spread out their bedding in the living room. Once Ben had to make himself a nest in a tiny hallway, with his socks jammed under the front door to keep out the draught. In fact, renting a house was very like camping, except the tent was made of stone or brick and didn't have to be put up and then taken down again.

She and Amy were best friends – so much so that once, when they were both six, and there had been some talk of Amy's parents emigrating to Canada, they had tied themselves together with bungee ropes and insisted they must never be parted. The plans to emigrate had been cancelled. This was not, in fact, because of the disturbing sight of a two-headed four-legged child cocooned in blue and black elasticated string. It was because Amy's parents got cold feet about leaving family and friends to start again among strangers. Even so, it made the friendship seem extremely powerful.

Even though Amy's family hadn't left the UK, they had moved. They were now too far away for Amy and Katie to go to the same school – and too far to visit unless they stayed overnight – all of which made the half-term get-together even more important.

Not that she and Amy were the only ones who'd have a good time. Everyone else would as well. Ben enjoyed hanging out with Amy's brother Sam. Amy's parents were good fun. And her own parents seemed to lighten up when they were all together. There was always a lot of laughing.

Katie spelt all this out in a voice that sounded horribly whiney, even to her own ears.

'I know,' said her mother. 'But I'm not going this time and that's it. I'll go at autumn half-term.'

'I should hope so,' said Katie. 'I wouldn't want to think we were going to miss two trips in a year.'

'Come on, Katie,' said her father. 'Ben's OK about it and he's younger than you.'

'Well, but that's Ben, isn't it?' said Katie. 'He's always OK about everything. He just goes with the flow. Anyway, Ben doesn't really think about things till they happen. I do! I look forward to things, and I've been looking forward to this ever since we got back last *October.*'

'I keep saying . . .' said her mother, '. . . none of you has to miss out. I'll enjoy having the house to myself for a while.'

Katie looked at her father. 'So can we go without her, then?' she asked.

He was walking out of the room as she spoke, heading for the garage for some reason.

'Can we go?' she said, following.

'I didn't think you'd expect me to answer that,' he said. He held the door between the house and garage open for her, and then lifted Ben's bike down from the wall hooks that supported it.

'It was a question,' said Katie. 'Why wouldn't I want an answer?'

'You really think we're going to go away for a week and leave your mother on her own?' He didn't look at her. He was pushing the bike to and fro, testing the brakes.

Katie didn't like the road she was going down, but she didn't know how to find a way off it. It was a strange feeling, like free-falling.

'Mum doesn't mind,' she persisted.

'You believe that?'

Katie frowned, suddenly distracted by the sight of the brake-blocks on Ben's bike being carefully adjusted. 'When are you going to check *my* bike?' she said.

'After this one.'

'Why are you doing Ben's first?'

'It was nearer.'

There was no arguing with that, it was so obviously true. Katie abandoned the lesser annoyance for the greater, the one that was filling her mind.

'So what are we going to tell the others?' she said.

'That we've got stuff we have to do that week.'

'But the house is booked already, isn't it?'

'We'll still pay our whack. They'll have more space than usual, that's all.'

However relaxed and easy-going a family is, there are still invisible lines that shouldn't be crossed. Katie knew she was moving steadily up towards one of them, but she couldn't stop herself. She took a deep breath and crossed it.

'Why don't we tell them the real reason?' she asked.

Her father didn't answer. He had prodded each tyre thoughtfully and now he was attaching the pump to the rear one.

All that was needed to step back over the line was to keep quiet, but Katie found she couldn't even do that. 'Why don't we tell them the truth?' she said loudly.

'There's no need,' said her father, pumping air into the tyre and then pinching it again.

'There *is*. They're our friends. Why do we have to pretend?'

No answer. He just screwed the cap back on the valve in silence.

'If you won't tell them, I *will*.'

She turned to go, but he was faster. Standing between her and the door, still holding the pump in one hand, he said, very quietly, 'You need to learn something about family loyalty.'

Katie pushed past him. She didn't like the expression on his face, but she knew, even without thinking about it, that he would never hit her. Just perhaps despise her a little, which was more painful.

'Well I think it's stupid,' she said.

He turned back to the bike. 'You think everything's stupid that doesn't have you centre-stage,' he said.

It was a few days later that Amy rang. She didn't get to the point right away, she talked about TV soaps for at least five minutes, then she lowered her voice slightly and said, 'Can anyone your end hear this conversation?'

'No,' said Katie. She was lying on her bed with the cordless telephone, and though her door was open she was sure there was no one else upstairs.

'OK,' said Amy, 'listen . . . I don't think I'm meant to tell you this, but my mum's worried that she's upset your mum.'

'Why would she think that?'

'Because you're not coming away with us. Has she upset your mum, do you know?' When there was no immediate answer, she went on, 'Because if she has she doesn't know what she's done, so she can't sort it out. But if you tell me what it is I can tell her and we can get it all OK again.'

Katie picked up a cushion with her free hand and began to stroke the fringe. She gave an enormous, exaggerated sigh. 'It's not your mum's fault,' she said. 'It's not anything any of you have done. All the problems are this end, believe me.'

'So what is it?' said Amy. Her voice was concerned, not curious, and for a moment Katie almost told her. But only almost.

'Is it really that she's got so much stuff to do?' Amy persisted.

'So she says.'

'The other thing Mum thought,' said Amy, 'was that it might be because of the accident. Like – maybe she's lost her nerve for going in the car?'

'No, she goes in the car,' said Katie. 'And she wasn't even *in* the car when she had the accident.'

'I know that. I know she was just crossing the road. But it must have given her a real shock, Katie. And it must have hurt a lot.'

Katie remained silent.

'Are you sure it isn't to do with that?' Amy persisted. 'Because it has to be something. I don't buy all this "stuff to do" thing. Stuff to do's never stopped her before. Maybe she really isn't over the accident yet.'

'She is,' said Katie. 'Course she is.' Believe it to be true, she thought, and it will be true. 'She's fine. Her arm mended really well. They took the plaster off really quickly. And she's nearly through with the physio sessions. She has the last one on Friday – just before we were *supposed* to leave.' She wound the cushion fringe so tightly round her finger that it hurt. They didn't want her to tell the real reason? They wanted her to pretend things were normal? All right, then, she would. 'She's perfectly fine,' she said, 'absolutely, totally fine. She's just being a major pain in the neck, that's all.'

She shook the fringe free and the cushion fell off the bed. As it bounced in the direction of the door, her eyes followed it, and she saw her mother, framed in the doorway. She had a mug of tea in one hand, and a look of hurt on her face such as Katie had never seen before.

'I have to go,' said Katie. She switched off the phone and sat up.

'I brought you some tea,' said her mother unnecessarily. She walked in and put the mug on the bedside table, shoving some bracelets out of the way with her other hand. The look had left her face, which was now completely blank.

I'm so sorry, thought Katie, I am so *very* sorry. But she couldn't say it. Her mother picked up the cushion, put it back on the bed, and went out of the room. Katie could hear her walking downstairs.

She grabbed the cushion and hugged it, her knees drawn up to her chest, her eyes tightly shut to stop the tears. What can they expect, she thought. I'm supposed to act as if nothing's wrong – they're asking too much – I have to be allowed to talk to someone, don't I? I have to be allowed to talk to my best friend.

She looked across at the rabbit-faced clock on the wall. It had hung there since she was very small, and it had always seemed to her to wear a friendly, kindly expression. Not now, though. Now it looked coldly down at her as if it didn't like her much. She tried to think it was only because the time was twenty to five and so the hands were the shape of a down-turned mouth. But it had been twenty to five many times before – and anyway it wasn't the mouth that seemed to dislike her, it was the eyes.

Despite the disapproving clock she stayed in her room for a couple of hours. No one called her until Ben got back from football practice.

Then she walked downstairs extremely casually and sat at the table. Ben was in a particularly good mood, and talked almost non-stop about strategies and positions. No one else would have had a chance to say anything anyway, so the fact that Katie and her mother were very quiet wasn't noticed.

That night the scream didn't come until about half-past four, but it was as loud and anguished as ever, ending on a long drawn out note, like the desperate cry of an animal in a trap.

Katie sat up in bed, her heart thumping, her hands over her ears, tears running down her face. 'I'm telling Amy the truth tomorrow,' she whispered to herself. 'I have to . . . I have to . . . I have to . . .'

THREE

This time Katie was more careful. She avoided the house phone and made the call on her mobile, sitting on the low wall outside the library on her way home from school.

'I can't talk long,' she said, when Amy answered. 'My battery's low. Sam took ages to find you.'

'Sorry – I was putting out the rubbish. You OK?'

'Yes, but . . . look, I'm not meant to tell you the real reason we're not coming, but I have to. It's driving me crazy. And it's not fair that your mum thinks it's her fault. You can tell them all, but none of you must ever let on that you know. Yes?'

'What *is* it?' said Amy, sounding alarmed.

'Mum has nightmares and she wakes herself up screaming. And she wakes the rest of us as well. And she won't come away because she'd be embarrassed if it happened when you're in the same house with us. And it might. In fact it probably would. It happens at least two or three times a week.'

'Is that *it*?' said Amy. 'But if you guys can go back to sleep again afterwards, I'm sure we can.'

Katie gave a dry little laugh. 'You haven't heard the screams,' she said. 'Honestly, I don't know why the neighbours haven't called the police . . . or the RSPCA. She sounds more like an animal being tortured than anything else.'

'That's awful,' said Amy.

The sympathy in her voice made Katie almost tearful. 'It *is*,' she said. 'It really is. Even though I know it's nothing it still gives me a horrible fright and often I lie there shaking for ages afterwards.'

'Oh yes.' Amy's voice was crisp. 'It must be nasty for you as well, but I meant it must be awful for your poor mum.'

'Oh,' said Katie. 'Yes, I suppose it is.' Then the irritation came back. 'But she won't *do* anything about it, or see anyone about it. And my dad just says it'll wear off. But I'm not convinced. It started a week after the accident, and it doesn't seem to be getting any less. It happened again last night.'

'She dreams the accident again, does she?' said Amy, her voice a little fainter. 'Crossing the road . . . the car hitting her . . . ?'

'I expect so.'

'Can't she even bear to tell you that?'

Katie hesitated. She found she didn't want to admit that she'd never asked. Her mobile gave a plaintive little bleep. 'It's going to cut us off in a minute,' she said.

'Listen,' said Amy urgently, 'if she won't do anything, and your father isn't doing anything, and Ben . . .' Somehow the mobile phone managed to communicate Amy's shrug. '*You're* the one who has to help her,' she said firmly.

'What am *I* supposed to do?' said Katie, startled.

'I'm not sure . . . But your dad's just waiting for it to go away – and if I know Ben, he probably sleeps through it.'

11

'He does sometimes.'

'So it has to be you. I think you have to make her talk about it.'

'She wouldn't want to.'

'K, don't be negative. She might, if it's just between you and her. Listen, I won't tell the others. Not if she doesn't want anyone else to know. It wouldn't be fair. Try it. It could help her just to talk . . .'

Ironically, the phone cut out on the word 'talk'.

Katie switched it off and snapped it shut. She stood up from the cold, hard wall and headed for home. She had wanted sympathy from Amy, not instructions and implied criticism. The conversation had unsettled her, and not just because it had ended on a power failure. She could remember exactly what she had said and exactly what Amy had said. She could remember their different tones of voice. She could spin the whole thing through her head again, like replaying a disc. In fact she couldn't stop it replaying, and each time the same thing was horribly obvious. She sounded like a sulky child and Amy sounded like an adult.

Why should her mother be willing to have a serious conversation with someone who sounded like a whining six year old?

It isn't easy to change a mood in a single moment. It can be done, but it's really hard. It's helpful if there's some mechanism to activate, some reason, however contrived or artificial, to account for the change.

Katie got home almost two hours before her father was due back from work. Ben was out at yet another football practice. She went straight upstairs, largely ignoring her mother who was sitting at the kitchen table paying bills.

In her room she looked out her new trousers and her best top. She kicked off her school shoes and slid her feet into the smarter ones she kept for special occasions. Then she brushed her hair, sprayed perfume into a cloud in the air and reversed into it, for an all-over effect, and pushed as many bracelets as she could find on to her left wrist. Finally, she picked up her mini tape recorder, checked the battery and marched downstairs again.

'Look at you!' said her mother, her hands resting on an open cheque-book. 'You look terrific. Where are you going?'

'I'm about to conduct an interview,' said Katie.

'Who are you going to interview?'

Katie sat down opposite her, switched on the tape recorder with a confident little click and set it on the table between them.

'I should like to interview you, Mrs Cole,' she said in her most formal voice. 'I do hope you're willing to cooperate.'

Her mother began to laugh. 'What *is* this?' she said. 'Is it a school project or are you just fooling around?'

'The first question I'd like to ask, Mrs Cole,' said Katie, 'is, do you have feelings of anger about the man who ran you over?'

The smile left her mother's face. She answered slowly, 'Of course not. It wasn't his fault. I wasn't paying attention and I walked right in front of his car.'

'But, Mrs Cole,' said Katie, 'surely you must wish he'd stepped on his brakes?'

13

'He did!' said her mother. 'He probably saved my life. And just for the record, *Ms Interviewer*, he didn't "run me over", he only knocked me down. I fell against a bollard and broke my arm. The car itself only bruised me.'

'And have you suffered any unpleasant after-effects from the accident?'

'Katie,' said her mother, 'where is this going?'

'You're avoiding the question, Mrs Cole,' said Katie, keeping her formal voice steady.

'Is this really for school?' said her mother. 'Do you have to tape me? You know I hate the sound of my own voice – that's why I always make your father . . .'

Katie raised her eyebrows. 'You mean Mr Cole?' she said coolly.

'. . . Sorry, Ms Interviewer, I should have said "my husband". That's why I always ask *my husband* to record the outgoing message on the answer-machine.'

They were looking each other straight in the eye, almost without blinking. Without dropping her gaze, Katie reached out and switched off the machine. 'Very well,' she said, 'this interview can be off the record. Have you suffered from nightmares since the accident?'

There was a pause. Her mother looked steadily at her in silence, and then seemed to come to a decision.

'Yes,' she said simply.

'Such bad nightmares that you wake up screaming?'

'Yes.'

'May I ask, Mrs Cole, if you have asked for medical help for this condition – and if not, why not?'

Her mother snorted. 'What could a doctor do? Give

me sleeping pills? Very nice! I might not wake up so easily. I might be stuck in it for even longer.'

'And in this dream, you relive the accident, right?'

Another pause. Her mother dropped her gaze and looked down at her own hands, resting on the pile of bills and signed cheques. 'No,' she said quietly. 'The dream has no connection with the accident at all – except . . .' She reached across and touched her lower arm, where the break had been.

'Except what?'

Her mother sighed and looked her in the eyes again. 'Except that it only started *after* the accident. And except that in the dream my arm hurts badly, where I broke it. But – in the dream – my arm isn't broken. It hurts because someone has hold of me, really tightly, in that same place. Katie – I have to know – what are you going to do with this information?'

'Nothing,' said Katie, in her normal voice. 'So is it always the same dream?'

'What was all that interview stuff?'

'I thought it might make you talk to me,' said Katie simply. 'And it worked, right? Don't stop now. *Is* it always the same dream?'

'Yes.'

'What happens?'

Her mother scooped the bills and cheques into a pile and got up. 'It's bad enough at night,' she said, 'I don't want to think about it in the day as well. It'll wear off – these things always do.'

'No, wait, don't go off somewhere,' said Katie.

Her mother hesitated, leaning on the table. 'Mrs Cole,'

said Katie, switching back to her interviewer persona, 'are your family sympathetic?'

There was a pause. Then, 'I think so.'

'Your husband?'

'He's very patient about being woken up a couple of times a week. And he knows it'll pass, just as I know it will.'

'Your son?'

'He's a sound sleeper. He often sleeps through it. The first time he actually heard me call out he came to our room, but we told him everything was all right and he's fine about it now.'

'And your daughter?'

Her mother sat down again. 'My daughter thinks I'm a major pain in the neck,' she said flatly.

'I *don't*,' said Katie. 'Mum, I'm sorry, I know you heard me say that – but it isn't the nightmare that gets me, it's you not talking about it or *doing* anything about it. Have you told anyone the dream?'

'No.'

'Not even Dad?'

'I haven't told anyone. Other people's dreams aren't interesting, and this one doesn't even make sense.'

'Tell *me* then. Come on, Mum, it might break it if you tell it. You said it's not about the accident – so what happens? No car? No being knocked down in the road?'

Her mother put the bills and cheques down again. She leant her elbows on the table and cupped her hands around her face, shutting herself away. 'Oh – other things,' she said, 'completely different things. It's all nonsense.'

'Tell me.'

'I can't . . . it's just a jumble . . .'

'But always the same jumble?'

Her mother kept her hands around her face, like a shield. 'Yes.'

Katie waited.

Then, 'There's a lot of noise,' said her mother, at last. 'I don't know what all of it is. I know there's shouting. I'm wet and cold. I'm *really* wet and there's water on my face and I feel I can't breathe. I look up and there are black things in the air above me – lines – I don't know what they are – they might be snakes. And then a man comes at me – he kind of swoops towards me – it's hard to see, it's a jumble of light and dark, but I see his hand shoot out and grab me by my arm. He's pulling me by my arm, dragging me – holding so tight and pulling so hard it feels as if he'll pull my arm right off. And I see his face, coming at me, and he's shouting, and his mouth is so wide open I think he might be going to swallow me. He's so *big* – his face, his hand, the great bulk of him – and I can't get free and I can't breathe properly and I think I can't scream – but I can – I *can* scream, and so I do, as loudly as I can – And then I'm sitting up in bed and your father's holding me and telling me it was a dream, and I think I hear the echo of my own scream dying away. I think it must be very loud.'

She took her hands away from her face. Her eyes were full of tears. '*Is* it loud?' she said.

'It's loud,' said Katie. She got up, walked round the table and put her arms round her mother.

'Just as well number 6 is empty and number 10 is deaf,' said her mother in a muffled voice.

They hugged for a moment. Then her mother pushed Katie gently away and stood up. 'So that's it,' she said. 'It's not about the accident, and it isn't about anything else either. It's meaningless, like most dreams. But I can't go away until I know it's over. I can't disturb other people. I feel such a fool. It's so childish.'

'I'm glad you told it,' said Katie. 'It's easier to understand now.'

'And now let's forget all about it, OK? Maybe you're right, and telling about it will have taken it away. Maybe we've all heard the last screams in the night, yes?'

That night the scream woke Katie at about half-past three. It was only one scream and it was over quite quickly, but it sounded as desperate as ever. I've made it worse, Katie thought. It's never happened two nights running before – I've made it worse, *now* what?

FOUR

Two of the shells fell, and both broke in different ways. The smallest of the collection, the Banded Venus, whose hinge had remained intact for all these years, separated into its two component parts. Worse, the pointed top was chipped off the prettiest, the Painted Topshell, so that the chambers inside, where the animal had once lived, were visible. Still, the Periwinkles and Necklace shells remained safely in their places, and so did the Slipper Limpets, like little single-seater row-boats, and the big Whelk shells.

The woman always tried to be too quick, that was the trouble. She was so impatient. She slammed around with the vacuum cleaner, whacked about with the duster, and then was gone. It was a wonder nothing had got broken before.

He put one of the large Whelk shells to his ear. The hearing-aid made the sea sounds louder, but it also made them stranger, like music from another culture, another time . . .

FIVE

It was worse, but it was also better. The dream might be striking more frequently, but at least, thought Katie, her mother would talk about it now. So would her father and so, surprisingly enough, would Ben. And the rabbit clock had recovered the benevolent expression it had worn throughout her childhood.

They each had their own ideas, but Amy was the only one who came up with the unthinkable suggestion – although that wasn't until much later.

This most recent time, the dream didn't hit until almost five-thirty in the morning, and one way and another no one got back to sleep again afterwards – not even Ben who, his father once said, would win a Gold if the Olympics had Sleep as an event. So everyone was up early and, a rarity on a school day, sat around the kitchen table, all eating cereal at the same time.

Sarah Cole looked strained and tired, but for the first time since it all started she wasn't wearing the closed-off expression that had made Katie so irritated with her.

'What I can't understand,' she said, pushing a bowlful of soggy flakes away from her, 'is why I don't know it's only a dream while I'm having it. Usually I *do* know. I may not be able to stop other dreams, but at least I don't take them seriously.'

'Yeah, well . . .' said Ben, 'this one's pretty dramatic, right?'

'I've told it to all three of you now,' said his mother, 'so you'd think when it starts again I'd remember talking about it and I'd know it wasn't really happening . . .'

'No, because it's a recurring dream,' said Katie. 'It's a repeat. You didn't know it was just a dream the first time, so you never will know, because it repeats the pattern exactly, and you not knowing it's a dream is part of the pattern.'

'She's right,' said Ben. 'It's in a different compartment in your mind. It's like – you're in one room while you're experiencing it, and then you're in a completely different room when you're talking about it.'

Dave Cole tipped the last of the tea into his mug. 'It has to have been set off by the accident,' he said, 'because of when it started. I just find it so peculiar that nothing in it seems to relate to what actually happened.'

'It *must*, though,' said Katie. 'Mum, do you think you're reliving it but your brain's changed the story a bit?'

'Dreams are like that,' said Ben. He'd been rocking back in his chair. Now he leant forward and the two front legs hit the floor with a thud that made them all jump. 'I had a really strong dream before a match one night. I was trying to walk along a cliff path – well, it was only a ledge really – and it was very narrow, and the ground was crumbling away and splashing down into the sea way down below. And then I realised I wasn't walking along the edge of the mainland, like I'd thought, I was walking out along a promontory. And when I looked behind me I could see that the sea had cut off

21

the promontory and I was stranded. And I knew my only chance was to climb down the cliff face and try to wade back to the mainland, but I had to be quick because the tide was coming in and soon it would be too deep . . .' He paused.

'And?' said Katie.

'And I woke up. I didn't yell, but I did feel really scared for a second.'

His mother shivered. 'I don't like that,' she said. 'It's the kind of situation you might get yourself into in real life.'

'I would not! I'm not daft!'

'But, Ben,' said his father, 'what's your point?'

'Oh,' said Ben. 'Well, just that it was an anxiety dream, right? I was really worried about the match the next day. It was after I had that chest infection thing and missed some practice and I was afraid I wasn't good enough to play. I was afraid I'd mess up. And that's what caused the dream. I got that right away. But the dream didn't have a pitch in it, or players, or a ball, or anything at all to do with what it was *really* about.'

'Yes,' said his mother slowly, 'I see what you mean. But . . .'

'In my mind,' said Ben, 'there was "suppose I'm going into something I can't handle?" And then in my sleep my brain showed me a vision of something I definitely wouldn't be able to handle. Right?'

'But it's different – it's entirely different.'

'Of course it is, Mum,' said Katie. 'He's him and you're you.'

'What I mean is – Ben's dream had a plot. It was the wrong plot, but it was *a* plot. It made sense. He knew what was happening, he knew what the danger was. And I agree, it probably *was* triggered by anxiety about the match. But mine doesn't have a plot, it doesn't have a story. It makes no sense at all. While I'm in it I have no idea what's going on. It isn't the same as Ben's at all.'

'I just dream better stories than you do,' said Ben cheerfully.

'The more we talk about it, the sillier it seems. You won't tell anyone else, will you? Any of you?'

Dave Cole looked pointedly at his daughter. Katie looked away. He got up and refilled the kettle. 'Maybe we'd better drop it for now,' he said, clunking the kettle on to its base and pressing the switch. 'We're getting a bit worked up here.'

'No one's getting worked up,' Katie began indignantly. Then she followed the direction of her father's look and saw her mother's expression.

But Ben ploughed on. 'I bet you've got the image of the accident playing on a loop-tape,' he said, 'but your brain's changed it a bit. Was there scaffolding on one of the buildings near where it happened?'

'Scaffolding?' said his mother. 'I don't think so, why?'

'You said there were lines in the air. They could be scaffolding. And the man bending over you could be a paramedic.'

'The man's shouting at her, Ben,' said his father. 'Paramedics don't yell at accident victims.'

'And there's no scaffolding,' said Katie. 'I go that way to school sometimes, and there isn't any, not anywhere.'

'OK, not scaffolding then. But I bet there's something.'

Katie's mother stood up and gave a determined tug at

the two ends of her dressing-gown belt, as if she was closing it and the conversation at the same time. 'You're never going to work out the meaning of something that doesn't *have* a meaning,' she said. 'I'm going to get dressed. And tonight you should all start thinking about packing. You'll have to leave early on Saturday so you've only got a couple of evenings to sort everything.'

'But we're not going, are we?' said Ben, as she went out of the room.

'No, we're not going,' said his father, with finality, adding a teabag to the pot and pouring the boiling water on to it. 'She won't, so we're not. End of story.'

Katie went upstairs. All the irritation had gone now. Instead she felt almost excited. It had become a mystery that she wanted to solve, and she felt sure she knew the next move. In fact it seemed so obvious she was surprised Ben hadn't thought of it as well. But there wasn't anything she could do until much later in the day.

When the time came, she took up her position outside the shoe shop as it closed.

'This is a nice surprise,' said her mother, as she double-locked the door. 'It's ages since you've walked me home.'

'I've come to walk you past the scene of the crime, Mrs Cole,' said Katie, and felt faintly guilty as her mother's smile faded.

'There wasn't a crime.'

'I know. But we can go and look anyway, can't we? It might help.'

It was about then that Katie realised she had never really known much about the accident at all. She simply hadn't been interested. It was over and her mother was all right, more or less – that was all she'd cared about. Now it felt strange to be trying to relive it, at second-hand and weeks later – strange but, surprisingly, quite nice.

Sarah Cole hadn't walked the quick way home from the shop that evening. Instead she had gone the long way, all up the High Street, past the station, then turned right into the shopping mall. There she'd gone into the stationer's, which always stayed open till six, and bought a ring binder and a two-for-the-price-of-one pack of refill pads Ben needed for school. This brought her out of the mall at the far end, which meant it was quicker to turn right again and walk the third side of the square than go back the way she'd come.

She'd taken a final right turn, down a side street, which led back to the High Street, and which came out a block below the shoe store. From there all she had to do was duck up the usual side street and turn left at the end to get home. Though of course, approaching from this direction, she needed to cross the High Street first – and that was when it happened.

Katie insisted they do the whole circuit again, rather than go straight to the disastrous crossing place. So, even though the light was fading and the wind was chilly, especially in the streets that ran north–south, that was what they did.

Traffic in the High Street was steady and quite brisk, much as it had been on the evening of the accident. They stood side by side on the kerb, and Sarah Cole rested her hand on top of a metal bollard beside her, one of a series designed to stop people parking cars half on the narrow pavement. 'This is what broke my arm,' she said.

'But it's *this* side. I thought you were crossing the road.'

'I'd just begun. I stepped straight out without looking. I sensed the car at once. Now I think about it, I remember I felt the heat of the engine. I tried to turn back, and he braked, but he bumped me as I turned and I fell really awkwardly and caught my arm on the bollard. I felt the bone go. Here, just above the wrist.'

'Yes, I do know which bit of you got broken,' said Katie. She made a face. 'It must have hurt. And it must have been very frightening.'

'It was more frightening for the driver I think. He insisted on calling an ambulance on his mobile, though really I could have made my own way to Casualty. Yes, it hurt, but mostly I just felt so silly. I still do – I still can't believe I was so stupid. How long have I been crossing roads? How *could* I just step off the pavement? Why didn't I look where I was going?'

'Yes, why didn't you?'

'I don't know.' Then she made a face. 'Oh yes I do,' she said. 'Something distracted me.'

'What?' said Katie, so eagerly that her mother laughed.

'Nothing interesting,' she said, 'and nothing I've dreamt about since. It was just that.' She pointed across the road. 'Just that stupid ad.'

The shop immediately opposite them was a newsagent, with a variety of ads covering most of the window and all of the door.

'Which stupid ad? There are millions.'

26

'Sweet Memories,' said her mother, with a sneer. 'Satin Pillows.'

It was in the centre of the top half of the door, at eye level to most approaching shoppers. The words Sweet Memories were in fake handwriting, with huge, looping, lilac-coloured letters that swept across the whole top third of the poster. Underneath was what looked like a pile of pastel, multi-coloured cushions heaped in a bowl.

'What are they?' said Katie, screwing up her eyes to focus better.

They crossed the road, looking both ways first with exaggerated caution, and went up to the door.

'Sweets,' said Katie, puzzled. 'Candy. You don't even much like sweets.'

'I hated those,' said her mother. 'I'd forgotten all about them till I saw this. They were still around when I was a child, and then they vanished. They really belonged to the days before my time when you bought sweets out of a big jar instead of pre-packaged. I think they just about hung on in a few small shops until I was about – oh, I don't know – seven or something. Then they disappeared. They were always called Satin Pillows, so Sweet Memories must mean they've revived them. Trying for the nostalgia trade.'

'Right,' said Katie, pushing open the door. 'We'd better buy some.'

Her mother followed her in, a little reluctantly, and watched as Katie bought a transparent package with about a dozen sweets and a lot of air inside it.

'Katie,' she said, as they walked on towards home, Katie struggling to break open the pack and finally succeeding in ripping a corner, 'I think you may be taking this psychoanalysis thing a bit too far.'

Katie passed the packet. Her mother hesitated then picked out a shiny pink cushion. Katie selected a green one.

After a brief silence, Katie said, 'They're all right. What's wrong with them? This one's lime – I quite like it.'

'This one's strawberry,' said her mother, trying not to dribble. 'Or raspberry. Or syntheticberry. It doesn't taste of much and the corners are sharp.'

'You're just not someone who likes sweets,' said Katie. She turned and looked back at the road they'd just crossed. There was no scaffolding, no telegraph wires, and no lines in the air. There was no film poster of a shouting man, and nowhere a film poster could have been. The only posters anywhere were in the newsagent's and they were all to do with sweets or water ices, except for the little handwritten cards about second-hand furniture and lost cats.

'Can we go home now?' said her mother.

Katie crunched into the hard coating on the lime-green satin cushion, pressed the soft centre against the roof of her mouth with her tongue, and nodded.

Later, talking to Amy on the phone, she said, 'I'm glad we did it, but it was a wash-out.'

And that was when Amy suggested it. 'I've been thinking,' she said. 'She told you the man in the dream was really big, didn't she? Well do you think it could be not so much that he was big but that she was really small? A child? Do you think the accident triggered a childhood memory?'

'It's possible,' said Katie slowly.

'I've seen your grandmother a couple of times,' said Amy. 'But I've never seen your grandfather – her father . . .'

'They split up when she was little.'

'How little?'

'I'm not sure.'

'Did he die?'

'I don't know. She's never said much about it. I asked once and she just said they broke up. And my gran's never said anything – but I suppose I've never asked her.'

'They could have split up over your mother,' said Amy's solemn voice, somehow made more important by the phone. 'Maybe your grandfather was horrible to your mother when she was little, and your grandmother left him for that reason. You know what I'm saying?'

'I think so,' said Katie. An unpleasant churning sensation was starting in her stomach and her mouth felt dry.

'I'm saying,' Amy went on, as if Katie hadn't spoken, 'the accident may have brought back a memory of something that *really* happened, years and years ago.'

'You mean her father shouted at her,' said Katie warily.

'It would have to be something much more horrible than that for her to suppress the memory for so long,' said Amy. 'What I'm saying is – maybe her father abused her.'

SIX

The underground train racketed through the tunnel, rocking slightly as it went. Katie sat near the door, reading the ads above the gently wobbling heads of the people sitting opposite her. Sweet Memories didn't feature here, she noticed.

Memories. What if memories, buried memories, weren't sweet at all? She didn't want to let the word Amy had used back into her head, but it was there before she could shut it out. Abuse. 'Maybe her father abused her,' Amy had said.

But after all, it was only a suggestion; it didn't have to be right. It just had to be checked out, that was all.

She looked around the carriage, searching for something else to think about.

It wasn't very full, which didn't surprise her. In fact she was more surprised there was anybody in it at all in the middle of a weekday morning. Who were they? Where were they going? Possibly they were wondering where she was going.

I just need to visit my grandmother, she thought, nothing odd about that. Except, of course, that there was something odd. No one knew she was making the journey – not her parents, not her brother, not even her grandmother. And no one knew she'd bunked off school, except Nicola who'd agreed to take in a note about a fictitious dentist's appointment.

Katie had made no attempt to forge the note – she had just written it herself, saying she'd lost the original note from her mother and would be in later. She had found she didn't really like lying, but it was better than the alternative – phone calls to home to check where she was, her parents panicking, maybe even a police search.

The train slowed and stopped. The doors wheezed open. Two people got out and no one got in.

Perhaps it wouldn't ever have come to that, she thought, as the train rattled on down another narrow tunnel. Perhaps no one at school would have said anything. Perhaps they'd just have questioned her next day. Perhaps the note hadn't been necessary. Oh well, too late now.

She peered up at the map above the head of the woman opposite – two more stations to go.

She'd tried really hard to talk to her mother after the telephone conversation with Amy, but her mother had been vague and unhelpful. Katie had been very careful – she hadn't mentioned Amy's theory, she hadn't even referred to the dream, she had just started talking casually about her own father and then said, 'So if your dad wasn't around, who fixed your bike for you when you were my age?'

'I didn't have a bike when I was your age.'

'Do you remember him?'

'No.'

'How old were you when he left?'

'I don't know. Very young.'

'A baby?'

'I don't know, Katie. I'm not holding out on you, I just don't know.'

'Don't you ever wonder what he was like?'

'Not really, no.'

'Well *I* wonder. He was my grandpa. Didn't you ever ask Grandma?'

'No.'

'Why not?'

'Oh, *Katie*! When I was little it didn't occur to me to ask. I was used to not having a father around, it seemed normal to me – especially as several of my friends were in the same situation. Then later on, as I grew up, I could tell she didn't want to talk about him, so I never raised the subject.'

'How could you tell?'

'Sometimes other people would ask her things – Are you a widow? – What did your husband do? – things like that. And she always managed to let it be known she was divorced – without actually using that word – and that she didn't want to say any more. People respected that, and so did I. We don't all nag on the way you do. Now – enough! I'm not hassling her about what's past and that's it.'

I won't hassle her, Katie thought now, as the train pulled in at Chalk Farm station, but she might not mind talking to me, she might even enjoy being listened to.

Common sense told her that if her grandmother had wanted to talk to her family, or be listened to by them, she would visit them more often, or invite them over to her place more often. It wasn't as if north and south

London were really that far apart. But she put the thought away.

She walked along the platform and up to ground level, away from the strange mingled smells of diesel, electrical dust and sweat, and out on to the noisy street. And realised for the first time that she hadn't planned how to broach a subject that might be taboo. What was more, she hadn't even planned what to do if her grandmother was out when she reached the house.

Fortunately she wasn't out, although she was obviously planning to go out at any moment, and was clearly shocked to see Katie at her front door. Her coat was on but unbuttoned. Her art-bag was propped against the wall in the tiny hallway. Her coppery-coloured hair was piled on top of her head as usual, partly held in place with long-toothed combs, partly wisping around her face in long tendrils. Not for the first time Katie thought her grandmother looked almost the same age as her mother, and usually a lot more relaxed.

Not relaxed at the moment, though.

She reached out and caught Katie by the arm, pulling her inside with one hand and slamming the door with the other. 'What is it?' she said. 'What's happened? Are you all right?'

Once she understood that Katie hadn't suddenly been orphaned, or chased half across London by kidnappers, or expelled from school without warning, anxiety changed to anger.

'You gave me such a fright!' she said. 'You've never just turned up before. I thought something dreadful must have happened. *And* you almost missed me – I'm due at my art class in ten minutes. What possessed you? Do they know you're here?'

'I forgot to tell them,' said Katie, who had had a moment of inspiration just inside the front gate. 'I have to do a school project on grandparents, so I need to talk to you.'

Oh how easy it was to invent, she thought, once you got started.

'Why don't you ask your other grandparents? There are two of them.'

'I already have – and I need to do the assignment tonight.' She tried to blank out the thought that she was developing rather too complicated a set of lies.

Her grandmother looked at her watch. 'Well if you've really come all this way on your own,' she said, 'you'd better have a cold drink or something. I'll just have to skip the class. Come through – what do you want? Juice?'

'Thank you.'

'I'm sorry I didn't seem pleased to see you, love, but you gave me a real shock. What on earth do you want to know? It'd take fifty-six years to tell you my life story!'

'I don't need much,' said Katie, accepting the apple juice and chocolate biscuit. She was surprised to discover how hungry and thirsty she was, now she actually had food and drink in her hands.

She sat down in the upright fireside chair, keeping herself as upright as it was. She had never felt entirely comfortable with this grandmother and, in fact, had never been alone with her before. Her other grandparents were relaxed, easy to be with, and always pleased to see her. This grandmother was somehow more remote. She wasn't unfriendly, and she was generous with presents – well, with money anyway – but she always gave the impression she'd rather be somewhere else, with someone else. Quite likely she was one of those people who don't much like children – which Katie had always found hard to understand because they must have been children themselves, once.

'Mum can tell me about *you*,' she went on, 'but I have to know something about my grandfather and Mum doesn't know anything.'

'There isn't anything to know,' said her grandmother, sitting down opposite her on the red plush sofa. 'We left him when she was four – she certainly knows that much. We left and that's it. End of story.'

'But – what was he like?'

'He was a waste of space, if you must know.'

'You must have liked him once.'

Her grandmother said nothing. Katie guessed she was waiting for her to leave.

'Mum says you never told her anything about him,' she persisted.

Her grandmother sighed, rather exaggeratedly. 'She never asked,' she said. 'She wasn't interested.'

'Why did you leave him?'

'Because I couldn't stand it any more.'

'But why?'

'Katie, it's over and gone and forgotten. I never think about it and I don't want to start now. Anyway it isn't the sort of thing I can talk to a child about.'

'So – was it about sex?' To her annoyance, Katie felt a flush spreading over her face.

Her grandmother laughed. 'No, not sex. The other thing.'

'You mean violence?' said Katie, the shock sounding in her voice.

'No, no, no. Drink. Alcohol. Inability to say no to the next one, or the one after that, or the one after that. I walked out on him, and that's the truth.'

'Did he get violent when he'd been drinking?'

'No! What's this obsession with violence? Sex and violence, that's all anyone thinks about. There are other things in life. I left him because he got boring when he was drunk. Maudlin. Do you know what maudlin means?'

'No.'

'It means he cried and said he loved me, and he loved our daughter, and he loved the whole world, and he knew he was good-for-nothing but – sob, sob – he'd change, he'd reform, he'd make himself worthy of us. And then he'd have another drink. You probably can't imagine how boring it is listening to someone maundering on, repeating himself, not even able to speak properly because he's so drunk. Someone who can't listen because he's too drunk, and who can't remember anything anyone said, including anything he said himself, while he was drunk. *And* have you any idea how much it costs, keeping someone who drinks? No, of course not, you don't know how much it costs keeping anyone yet, but believe me, it's a lot.'

'Didn't he work?'

'Oh yes. Technically he wasn't an alcoholic – he could keep off it by day. Just as well – he was an electrician. But he didn't earn enough to pay the regular bills as well as the off-licence.'

'Is he still alive?'

Her grandmother looked startled. 'I've never wondered. He's in the past – he's gone – but I don't know if he's *really* gone.' Her expression softened. 'Stupid man, I should think he *is* dead by now if he went on drinking like that.' She hesitated. Katie waited. 'I did try to help him at first,' she said. 'I really did. But you can't, you see. Not if the person doesn't want to stop. And he was weak and indecisive. Drinking made him feel strong. It let him put off decisions. So he didn't really try to stop. We left, and I brought Sarah up here, to live in London.'

'I thought you'd always been here.'

'No. When I was married we lived in a dead-and-alive hole beside the sea.'

'Where?'

'It doesn't matter where. They're all the same. I've never been back. I prefer to think it doesn't exist any more, if you really want to know. They were *not* the happiest days of my life.'

'I'm sorry.'

'It was hardly your fault! You didn't exist then!'

Katie shook her head. She couldn't think how to explain she had been offering sympathy, not an apology. Funny language, English, she thought.

'The beach was all right, I suppose,' her grandmother went on grudgingly, 'or all right for a child, anyway. But it wasn't all right for me. And it wouldn't have been any good for her, either, as she grew up. There was nothing to do – and it's horrible living beside the sea.'

'Why?'

'It makes you feel as though you're at the end of everything.'

Katie had no idea what to say to that, so she said nothing, and a rather tense silence began to grow.

She hoped she'd remember, when she got home, how difficult it had been to interview someone so determined not to open up – how unthinkable even to touch on Amy's theory. She didn't feel as though she knew any more than she had when she arrived, but she couldn't think of anything to ask that might help.

Her grandmother broke the spell. 'Have you got your fare home?' she said.

The sense of failure must have shown on her face, Katie realised, because her grandmother reached across and patted her hand rather awkwardly.

'I'm sorry I haven't been much use,' she said, 'but they can't expect you to write about a grandfather you never met.'

Katie opened her mouth to speak and then closed it again. She had almost said 'Who can't?' For a moment she'd forgotten all about the invented project from school.

Her grandmother stood up suddenly, and Katie stood, too, assuming she was being dismissed.

But, 'Look, I'll let you see the photo album, such as it is,' said her grandmother. She pulled open the bottom drawer of a bureau in the corner and began digging through what looked like old theatre programmes. 'It won't be any use at all, but it's all I have to offer, I'm afraid.'

'Thank you,' said Katie, sitting down again and accepting a black-bound album on to her lap.

Opening it, turning the pages carefully, she realised that she had never seen a single photograph of her mother when she was very young. But here she was. There as a baby, in her mother's arms in a hospital bed. Then as a toddler, standing beside her mother at an open gate, the short garden path and small house blurring in the background, holding on to her mother's skirt with one hand and staring into the camera.

Next there was a glamorous, very posed, shot of a woman in a beautiful, floaty evening dress, her coppery hair – a little lighter and more golden than now – piled up in the familiar style, her eyes heavily made up – Grandma very young, lovely, and extremely pleased with herself.

Then a little cluster of three beach pictures – all concentrating on the same child – no longer a toddler, probably three years old. In one she was crouching, looking down at the shingle, one hand reaching out for something. In the next she was standing, feet firmly planted on the ground, looking straight at the camera with serious eyes and holding out a large shell on the palm of her small hand. In the third, she was sitting alone in a model lifeboat, which was mounted on some kind of base outside a lifeboat station. Probably it would rock to and fro if someone put money in a slot.

Although she was such a little girl, the solemn expression was very familiar, and so were the eyes. Poor little thing, thought Katie. Whatever happened to you to give you such terrible nightmares all these years later? I'm so much older than you. If I'd been there – but been there as I am now – I'd have been looking after you. Why are you so often alone? Why does no one hold your hand?

She turned the page and came on a blank – and then another.

She looked up, startled. 'Aren't there any more?'

'I can't stand family photos,' said her grandmother. 'I hate it when people have them out on show. It's as if the past's following them around. People should let go of the past and move on.'

The past does follow us around, Katie thought, but didn't say. What she did say was, 'There isn't a picture of my grandfather.'

'He was the one who always took the photos, that's why,' said her grandmother. 'Turn to the back.'

Katie leafed through several more empty pages and there, on the very last one, was a wedding photo. There was her young grandmother in a short, straight cream dress, with flowers woven into her hair, holding a small posy. Beside her stood a tall man in a suit who looked about ten years older than his bride. She was looking at the camera, laughing, and looking happier than Katie had ever imagined she could look. The man was looking down at her and he was laughing, too. Katie stared and stared at him. He looked so ordinary. Nice – and ordinary. Not at all like a man who could have done bad things. But then he didn't look drunk, either, yet clearly he often was.

'No pictures of him with my mother?'

'No. How could there be – he was behind the camera.'

You could have taken one, Katie thought, but again didn't say.

All the way back on the train Katie's mind was filled with the image of the solemn little girl. She must have often seen him drunk, she thought, if he really did drink that much. That could have been scary. But it seemed he wasn't violent, ever.

Was it possible to abuse a child without being violent? Could there be such a thing as gentle abuse – and might that be worse, creepier, altogether more sinister? And if there was a horrible secret in the past, how would it ever be possible to uncover it if the only people who might know about it were unlikely ever to admit it?

Or perhaps there was no secret, perhaps nothing bad did happen. Perhaps the dream really was meaningless, as grown-up Sarah insisted. Katie felt her mind clutching hold of that idea with immense relief. Yet, even as she began to relax, she was aware that, away in a tiny corner, something nagged . . . in the dream, Sarah was small. As small as a child.

In one way, Katie thought, she was no wiser than she had been before making the trip, but in another way she most definitely was.

The picture of the child outside the lifeboat station had been very clear, the lettering on the wall behind her, spelling out the town's name, very easy to read. The picture of mother and child at the open gate had been clear, too. There, on the gatepost, below her young grandmother's resting hand, was the house number. And there on the wall beside the gate was the street name. That was why the two – mother and small daughter – were posed where they were. The photographer – her grandfather – had obviously wanted to get the name and number in, so that the caption was contained within the picture itself. Just as well, because whoever had stuck those few pictures into the book had not bothered to write anything at all underneath them.

But because of those two pictures, Katie now knew where her mother had lived for the first four years of her life.

SEVEN

Perhaps here is where this story begins, with two people on a train, travelling to a south coast town not much more than two hours away. Such a short journey to get to someone's past.

Katie sat quietly, looking out of the window at the fat grey clouds, grouping and regrouping in the sky; and at the rain, slashing against the windows at an angle, like thin knives that melted on impact. Beside her, her mother had a book open. She was looking at the text in front of her as if she was reading it, but Katie noticed she never turned a page.

Amy had been adamant. 'You have to get her there,' she'd said, her voice crackling with urgency down the phone. 'She has to go and see her father.'

'He may be dead,' Katie had objected. 'And even if he isn't, he probably doesn't still live in the same house.'

'I bet he does,' Amy had said. 'From what your grandmother told you, he doesn't sound like the get-up-and-go type. Anyway, just seeing the place where it happened could give her the memory back properly so she can deal with it.'

'The place where *what* happened?' Katie had said, sharply. 'We don't know that anything did.'

'Something must have,' Amy had said simply.

The trip had been amazingly easy to arrange. It had

all happened so fast that Katie felt almost breathless, even though she was sitting still in the moving carriage. She wondered if her mother felt the same.

Both her parents had been cross when they'd discovered she'd lied at school. And neither of them had been happy to hear that she'd taken herself off to north London and doubtless stirred up unhappy memories for her grandmother who, it turned out, hadn't been told anything about the nightmares or the paralysing screams.

But, perhaps surprisingly, her suggestion that she and her mother should go away together for a week had appealed to her father.

'I like to see you getting on better with your mother,' he had told Katie.

'A mother-and-daughter bonding session,' the telephone voice of Amy had said with confidence, when she'd heard the news. 'He's right. It's a good idea of ours.'

That Friday, both Katie's parents had stopped work at lunchtime. Dave was still hoping to persuade his wife to agree to go to the holiday cottage on the Saturday. Sarah was still insisting they should all go without her. So they were both at home when Katie and Ben got back from school, Katie with her plan clear in her mind.

She had thought carefully before putting the idea forward. She was as sure as she could be that any suggestion of making contact with her grandfather would charge the whole idea with too much drama, too much emotion, and the trip would never happen. In the end she had simply suggested that her mother's birthplace might supply the key to the dream.

She had been careful not even to hint at the shadowy figure of her grandfather.

When Ben had asked why she was so sure the dream had come from the first four years of their mother's life, rather than from the rest of her childhood, in London, she was tempted to say, 'Because her father was around during those first four years,' but she didn't. She watched Ben to see if he would guess. Realistically, if there had once been a large man, dragging at little Sarah's arm and shouting into her face, the chances that he was her father were surely enormous. But Ben didn't seem to make the connection.

At once their own father had started talking enthusiastically about a nice break being good for stress, and Katie knew that he was simply picturing this as a pleasant mini-holiday. He was not complicating it by thinking of it as an attempt to find the truth.

Katie had watched her mother begin to say no. Then she had seen her glance at them all, and hesitate. Katie felt she knew exactly what was going through her mind. She didn't want to go – but at the same time she understood that if she refused then the rest of them wouldn't get away that week either. If she insisted on staying at home, they'd all lose out.

Katie looked at her now, sitting upright beside her, holding on to her book and staring at it as if determined to look like an average, relaxed traveller. She felt slightly guilty.

Looking back she could see that once she'd floated the idea, her mother had been cornered. In that moment of hesitation, when she didn't actually say no, everyone had sprung into action.

There was so little time. They had to call Amy's parents to say that Ben and his father would be joining them at the cottage in Wales after all; check train times to the South Coast; contact the Tourist Information Centre for the names of small hotels; book a twin room with a sea view; pack.

Any second thoughts or change of heart would have caused disruption and disappointment.

Cornered. That was definitely the right word for it.

Did I bully her? thought Katie. Do we all bully her? Has she been bullied her whole life, ever since . . . Ever since it happened, whatever and whenever it was?

They had a picnic about an hour into the journey – buttered buns, hunks of cheese and fat tomatoes that dribbled slime and pips when bitten into.

Afterwards, Katie sidled down the aisles, clutching at the backs of seats as the train rocked along on elderly tracks, and came back with a tea and an apple juice in covered beakers. Both slopped on the floor as soon as their plastic lids were snapped off.

'They're too full!' said Katie angrily.

'They're not now,' said her mother, and began to giggle.

Relieved, Katie felt herself relax. 'I didn't force you to come, did I?' she said.

'No, of course not. I just hope the rain lets up.'

'Do you think you'll recognise anything?'

Her mother shrugged. 'Can't tell. I shouldn't think so.

I can remember a beach, I think – sand . . . stones . . . shells . . . but that could have been a holiday beach somewhere else. I don't think I really remember much before I was about six or seven.'

Katie frowned. I can remember further back than that, she thought, why can't you? But her mother was looking out of the window, and if she guessed the silent question, she certainly didn't answer it.

The train was slowing down. Katie glanced at her watch. This was it. She felt a twinge in her stomach. Excitement? Fear?

Sarah stood up and began to pull her raincoat down from the rack. 'Just so long as you don't try to find my father,' she said conversationally, not looking at her daughter. 'If he's still alive, which he probably isn't, the shock would most likely kill him.'

She stooped and began to pull their bags out from behind the seat. 'And me,' she added lightly.

Katie said nothing.

The train slid into the station and stopped with a slight shudder. The few other people in the carriage shuffled towards the doors at either end and began to get out. Waiting until they'd all passed, so they could hitch their luggage on to their shoulders without hitting anybody, Katie and her mother were last.

Everything seemed to be grey – the tarmac of the platform, the faded paintwork on the carriages, the blank VDU screen which suggested no more train movements for some time, the glimpses of sky. The platform was covered but the rain slanted in under the roof and stung the sides of their faces.

'I can't see the sea,' said Katie. 'You'd never know we're at the coast.'

'Lick your lips,' said her mother, marching on ahead. 'You can taste the salt. Now that's something I *do* remember.'

Then she stopped, so suddenly that Katie almost collided with her. 'Did Grandma give you an address?' she asked sharply.

'No,' said Katie.

Her mother nodded, satisfied, and walked on towards the turnstile and the station concourse.

Not exactly, Katie added, but she didn't say the words aloud.

EIGHT

The small town seemed to be waiting for something –
the rain to stop, perhaps, or the season to begin.

It might be half term, but the weather was not likely
to attract day visitors. As for those who might stay longer,
most preferred to choose neighbouring resorts.

Family groups were drawn west along the coast to a
rival with a large modern leisure centre and swimming
pool, family restaurants, clubs, bars – and an aquarium
with a walkway between its vast tanks so that its
visitors could imagine they were exploring the sea floor,
surrounded by fish but, magically, still able to breathe.

Others found the resort to the east more appealing,
with its cliff-top and inland walks, opportunities for bird
watching, and numerous teashops and bookshops.

Here, it was hard to see much that was tempting.

Not the battered pier, its tiny theatre long since closed
down, the appeal of its slot machines lost on punters
accustomed to the variety and drama of computer
games.

Not the small arcades along the sea front, most of
which would stay closed until Easter. Not the tall, narrow,
dingy hotels which all looked closed even if they weren't.
Not the lifeboat station, halfway between the pier and
the cliffs, now retired from its intended purpose and
used as a small museum. And not even, apparently, the

chip shops, which were open but quiet, or the burger joints, or the shops selling novelty sweets in the shapes of seashells, and resolutely useless gifts.

At the older end of town to the east, built when fishermen still put out from the tiny sheltered bay under the cliffs – before the cliffs themselves began to disintegrate from above, filling the tiny harbour with rocks and threat – there was even less activity.

The last two boats were used for tourist trips along the coast on clear days during summer. Now, though, they were drawn above high water, tied down and securely tarpaulined. The café, and the corner shop selling beach toys, ice creams, postcards and magazines, struggled to keep open all year round, saved by the old-town residents who liked a glimpse of the sea when they bought their cigarettes and stamps, or somewhere warm and companionable to drink tea on a winter's afternoon.

The cliffs that rose from the far end of the old town were deeply eroded and a fence along the top kept walkers well back from the edge. It was not until several miles on that the cliffs became stable enough for walkers to rejoin the coastal path in its proper place, at the rim of the land.

It was the time of the high spring tides, which meant there was less beach than usual. The sea was noticeably close in. It was also unexpectedly deep at the shoreline because it had spent much of the winter steadily pushing the shingle of its bed towards the land, piling it into a natural breakwater.

Below the ridge of shingle, the land dropped away

gently so that at low tide even a child could wade out a long way and still only be up to its waist in the water. But now, at high tide, with the sea gnawing at the top of the heaped shingle bank, one step into the water would take a tall man out of his depth at once.

The whole body of water was moving, licking at the edge of its territory, but the wind had dropped and the tide had not yet turned so there were no waves; just a restless swell, which made the great grey expanse look like a living creature. Once, people believed in sea monsters that surged from the depths to devour the unwary. Now they knew that the monster was the sea itself. Sometimes at high water, especially at storm times when the onshore winds were fierce, it was possible to believe that it yearned to swallow the whole town.

Its spray was already eating the nearest buildings. The salt and damp were working their way in under the surface paint, lifting it off in thick wide flakes, as though lifting a piecrust to see the filling underneath. In the grey, rainy light the buildings that faced out to the horizon, with nothing between them and the ocean but the promenade and the shingle bank, looked almost like an extension of the flotsam and jetsam at the waterline; the plastic bottles, tin cans, sudden sharp shards of glass, splintered wood and tangled, acrid seaweed.

Perhaps it didn't only want to swallow the town, this hungry sea; perhaps it also wanted to feed on the people; perhaps especially the people. After all – they belonged to it. It had released them, aeons ago, to creep on to land, learn to breathe air, evolve lungs and limbs and become land-based animals, in all their various forms and types. But it never let them forget where they came from. The fertilised human egg always did, and always does, begin its life as a tiny fish-like creature, living in fluid. Even when it develops into human form, and emerges into the air all over again, mimicking its most ancient ancestors; even when it breathes and grows and stands, and begins a life lived entirely on dry land, still the legacy of the sea persists – in its salty sweat, its salty blood, its salty tears.

The girl standing close to the sea's edge, halfway between the pier and the beginning of the old town, had salt tears on her face – unless it was just the spindrift, hanging in the air, coating everything with sea-breath. She stood quite still, feet planted on the stones, looking out over the water – as if waiting for something.

On this bleak afternoon she was almost the only human presence along the whole length of the sea front. Almost but not quite. A woman and a teenage girl had cut through one of the side streets from the nearest bus stop and were walking past the small, closed arcades on the town side of the promenade. The bags they were carrying were large enough to suggest they planned to stay for several days. They paused outside a small hotel, so narrow and discreet it had been more or less invisible until they drew attention to it by beginning to climb the shallow stone steps to its front door.

They weren't talking so she didn't hear them, didn't look round, didn't see them struggle through the door and disappear inside.

They saw her, though, and scanned the surface of the sea, expecting to see a swimming dog retrieving a thrown stick. The sea was empty, which puzzled them briefly, but once they were inside Sea Spray Hotel, ringing the bell at the desk, they forgot about her – at least until later.

NINE

Katie dialled Amy's number as soon as Sarah disappeared into the shower-room and closed the door.

Amy sounded breathless. 'We've only just arrived,' she said. 'I'm supposed to be helping unload the car. Where are you? I can't hear waves or seagulls.'

'Still in the hotel room. First she insisted on unpacking everything and putting stuff away in cupboards and drawers and things. Now she's taking a shower – she never has a shower in the afternoon.'

'Delaying tactics,' said Amy.

'You think?'

'Of course. She's putting off going out in case she remembers something.'

'We've been out already. We got the bus from the station and then we walked to the hotel – but she doesn't recognise any of it.'

'Maybe she does but she's blanking it.'

Katie shook her head, and then remembered that, close though Amy sounded, she couldn't actually see her. 'No,' she said. 'She's not thinking that way. She doesn't connect the dream with this place at all.'

'Oh yes, she does,' said Amy firmly, 'whether she knows it or not. Otherwise why did she agree to go with you?'

'Oops,' said Katie, 'shower over. I'll call again.' She

switched off the phone and tucked it out of sight.

When at last they did leave the hotel, neither Katie nor Sarah had any idea where to go or what to look at first. Without comment, Sarah turned left, towards the old town.

'Why this way?' said Katie, keeping pace with her.

'Nicer view this way,' said her mother. 'We've got the cliffs in front of us instead of that old pier.'

They crossed the road on to the promenade and headed on east. And there it was, overlapping the prom ahead of them, its slipway sliding down the beach and disappearing under the water – the lifeboat station – immediately recognisable from the old photograph. It was closed and shuttered, and the coin-in-the-slot lifeboat ride outside had gone, but it was unmistakeable.

Katie stood on the weathered metal disc, set into the tarmac of the prom where the ride had once been, and looked at her mother for any sign of recognition or memory – but there was none.

'It says it's a museum,' she said, looking at the lettering on the door. Below the words 'Lifeboat Museum' hung a small notice headed 'Opening Times'. The names of the days had been printed on it in blue marker pen, but no one had written in any times.

Her mother paused, glanced at the square, wooden building, and then walked on. 'You should have gone to Wales with the others,' she said. 'You'll die of boredom here.'

'I'll be fine,' said Katie. How weird, she thought, following and then doing a little run to catch up. *I* know she's been in this exact spot at least once before, but *she* doesn't – she has no idea.

'Is any of this familiar yet?' she asked, glancing back at the lifeboat station, seeing it now from the same position as the photographer all those years ago. So now she was walking across the exact spot where her grandfather had stood, at least once.

'The sea always seems familiar, doesn't it?' said Sarah. 'I do remember the sea, but I think it's only because we've all been on beach holidays in various places. I don't think I'd be able to tell if it's this actual piece of beach and sea I remember or some other one.'

'What about the lifeboat place?' said Katie.

Sarah shook her head. 'Not specially,' she said. She turned briefly to look back at it. Then she shrugged. 'No, not at all,' she said.

They walked on in silence. It's just so strange, Katie thought. That little girl is lost – gone. She's evaporated away, with whatever terrified her. Yet she isn't really gone. She's walking beside me. And she's my mother.

The few cars that were on the move were all passing through. The ones travelling in their direction turned out of sight quite soon, following the road where it swung inland to skirt around behind the sweeping rise in the ground with its edging of crumbly cliff-face. Otherwise they were the only people out – apart from a couple walking a small black and white terrier on the beach. The dog was ignoring the sea, darting from one pile of flotsam to the next, nosing about in the hope of finding something interesting. It was the only lively presence in sight.

The promenade ended abruptly at a fence, a limited safety measure to prevent people walking on to the narrow beach below the cliffs. A notice warned of the dangers of falling rocks.

Just this side of the danger-zone there was another narrow slipway, covered in green slime. High up the beach above it the last two remaining boats slept under their covers, waiting for summer.

Opposite, near the corner where the narrow road turned north, was a small café. Through its steamy windows they could see three people, each sitting alone at a small table. The shop beside it looked closed, but turned out to be open when Katie tried the door.

It seemed almost shockingly colourful inside, after the greyness out of doors. There was a double-fridge covered in pictures of ice creams and lollies – a wall of shelves stacked with newspapers and magazines – another wall offering cosmetics, soap, toothpaste and, rather optimistically, sun creams. The window display was a disorganised pile of jelly sandals, inflatable armbands, sunglasses, beach balls and vividly patterned caps and hats. Crowding the space in the centre of the shop were three revolving stands, one with picture postcards, the second with greetings cards, the third with maps and booklets. There were cigarettes at the back of the counter, sweets on it, beach toys in front of it – but no one behind it.

'Why are we in here?' said Sarah. 'We don't need anything, do we?'

'I'm just looking around,' said Katie vaguely, drifting over to the stand with the booklets on it and revolving it as casually as she could. She knew exactly what she needed. It was something she'd had in mind since before they set out from home, but she had assumed she'd have to go right into the town to a proper bookshop to find it. Yet here it was, three copies of it, on the third rack of the third revolving stand – a local street guide, complete with map. She didn't pick it up at once, but waited until her mother turned to the newspaper display and began reading her way along the headlines. At much the same time a man appeared from the back of the shop and stood behind the till, smiling hopefully.

Katie picked up a roll of mints and held them out to him, together with the street guide. By the time her mother looked round, she had the mints and the change in her hand, and the guide was out of sight, in the pocket of her jacket. She wasn't ready yet to push the idea of seeking out the house in that crucial photograph, where her young grandmother stood eternally at the gate, little Sarah beside her, forever fixed in black and white gloss, holding a fistful of her skirt.

Right now, grown-up Sarah was holding a *What's On* listing. 'So there is a cinema in town, then?' she said to the man behind the counter.

'Indeed there is,' he said, enthusiastically. 'Three screens. Very small, though. You'll need to book if it's something popular you're interested in.'

'Are you sure?' said Sarah. 'The town doesn't seem to be overflowing with visitors.'

'Oh, there are plenty of people around. They just don't come down by the sea when the weather's a bit off, that's all. They'll be going round the shops.'

'Are there good shops here?' said Sarah.

He spread his hands, gesturing at his stock. 'You're already in one of the best!' he said. Then he lowered his hands, still smiling. 'I'm joking of course,' he said. 'Go to the shopping mall in the centre and you'll find most things you could possibly want. Or, if you're into antiques and second-hand books, go round the shops in the old town, back up from here. Where are you from?'

'London.'

'Oh, right. Well, we may not be able to compete with the Big City, but we're not bad. Not bad at all.'

Katie was back at the revolving stand with the booklets on it. She'd been in such a hurry to buy the street guide quickly and discreetly that she hadn't looked at anything else. 'What is there to do around here?' she said, glancing down the titles, 'apart from the cinema and the shops?'

The man behind the counter sighed. 'There isn't much exactly *here*,' he said. 'But go along the coast in either direction and you're spoilt for choice. Take a bunch of those brochure things – they'll give you some idea. This is a really good centre. You can get anywhere from this town. There's a bus map on that stand too – see it? – no, lower down – yes, that's the one. Go on, it's free.'

Katie folded it and put it in her pocket with the street guide. 'What about the Lifeboat Museum?' she said.

He shrugged. 'Very small,' he said. 'And John only opens when he feels like it.'

Katie picked up a booklet with 'Ghosts of the South Coast' in spiky lettering on its cover.

'Ah,' said the man behind the counter. 'You have to pay for that – it's only the brochures that are free. Have you got the one about the ice rink? And the aquarium? And there's a swimming pool, and lots of other stuff – but like I say, not exactly *here*.'

'So are there ghosts exactly *here*?' said Katie, turning *Ghosts of the South Coast* over and reading the list of places on the back.

'None in that.'

'Do you mean there are, but they're not in this? Or do you mean there aren't any at all?' said Katie. She put the booklet back. There didn't seem much point paying for something that only talked about other places.

He hesitated. Then, 'There's nothing to see,' he said.

'But – do you mean there *is* something?' said Katie, suddenly very alert. A whole new possibility had just come into her head. Had little Sarah seen a ghost all those years ago? Was it possible that the shouting man was actually a phantom – a phantom who'd terrified her in the past and had then come back to haunt her all over again years later?

'No, there isn't anything,' said the man behind the counter firmly. Then he seemed to waver. 'Just memories,' he added.

'Memories of *what*?' said Katie impatiently.

'Memories of the past.' He picked up a mobile phone from beside the till and began to dial. 'Is there anything else you need?' he said, polite still, but no longer chatty, no longer cheery. 'I have to put in my weekly order now or I'll miss the delivery.'

Sarah paid for the *What's On* listing, and they left in silence.

'Memories of the past,' said Katie sarcastically, when they were outside. 'What else would memories be of? The future? What was it he wouldn't tell us?'

'I don't think he was hiding anything,' said her mother. 'I think he was being deliberately mysterious to try and beef up our interest in this place. I have to say – I'm not surprised Grandma moved away!'

'Be fair,' said Katie, 'we've hardly seen anything yet.'

They crossed the road back to the prom, and as they started the return walk, Katie saw the battered old pier from a new angle, sideways on.

Distant though it was – a good ten or fifteen minutes' walk away, well beyond their temporary home in Sea Spray Hotel – its silhouette was very clear. There were the traditional domes on top of the main structure, two thirds of the way along it. There were the deck and landing stage at the far end, with the tiny figure of a line-fisherman leaning over the rail.

And there were the supports – long black legs which raised it above sea level and which, now the tide was going out, were standing clear of the water at the shore-ward end, so that the beach the other side could be glimpsed through them. But the supports were not simple straight legs, like the legs of a table – they had cross-braces and struts set between them. From here, the effect was as though someone had painstakingly drawn a pavillion and deck, and then furiously scribbled a fierce network of intersecting black lines underneath.

The dream had involved fear, water, a sense of being

unable to breathe – and mysterious black lines looping above.

Katie glanced at her mother – but her mother was looking out to sea, watching a flight of seabirds wheeling by.

On an impulse, Katie jumped down on to the shingle. 'Let's walk along the beach,' she said – and she began to do just that, knowing her mother would follow, feeling the hard shifting pebbles crunching under her shoes, deliberately aiming straight for the far-off pier, straight for the complexity of twisting, criss-crossing, sea-washed black lines.

TEN

When they first set out, Katie found it difficult not to walk too fast. It was so obvious that this had to be it. Wasn't that why her mother had chosen to walk away from the pier earlier – instinctively turning her back on a horrible memory?

She tried not to keep glancing at her, but to keep her eyes straight ahead, fixed on the jumble of black lines supporting the pier, which grew steadily larger as they drew steadily nearer.

'This is painful,' said Sarah, from a few steps behind her – and Katie looked back, startled, misunderstanding for a moment. But her mother only meant that the stones were uncomfortable to walk on, pressing through her thin shoes and bruising her feet.

'There's sand down here,' said Katie.

She began to trudge down the shingle bank, still wet from the receding sea, but the stones turned and shifted under her feet, growling and grinding against each other, rolling her steeply downwards. The only way to keep her balance was to run, so she did, and managed to stop just before the edges of the waves.

Sarah ran down the unstable bank behind her.

The narrow strip of sand was hard and wet. Every step made a shallow, shivering footprint that filled instantly with water and then disappeared.

Glancing over her shoulder Katie saw that her mother was walking backwards. 'Look,' she said lightly, 'I make no tracks.'

Soon, thought Katie, soon. Surely she'll realise – surely she'll remember.

She tried to avoid the thought that followed on, the thought that said – and then what? How will she react – how upset will she be – will I be able to look after her?

Closer and closer, with still no word of recognition from Sarah, until together they walked right up to the great metal supports and stopped in front of the nearest ones. They were covered in clusters of tiny, craggy grey barnacles that looked dead – fossilised, even – but almost certainly weren't.

'Do you want to walk underneath it?' said Sarah.

'Could do,' said Katie, watching her.

Sarah made a face. 'It looks even colder and danker under there than it is out here,' she said. 'Let's go up to the prom and walk round the front of it instead.'

Kate took two steps in under the pier. In the dim light of the bleak afternoon it was almost dark under there. 'Don't you remember?' she said.

Her mother joined her and they stood side by side, staring upwards at the construction of metal struts with the wooden boards of the pier's deck forming their roof. Lines of daylight showed between the boards.

'I don't remember ever being underneath here,' said Sarah slowly. 'But, do you know, I think I *do* remember being up on the pier and daring myself to look down through the gaps between the planks.'

She walked a little further under, looking up all the time.

Katie followed, and shivered. There were breaths of chill, damp, salty air drifting around them, picking up a faint scent of rusty metal and rotting seaweed as they passed.

'I *do* remember,' said Sarah, in a kind of triumph. 'It was scary, but in a nice way. I suppose I half thought I might fall through the gaps, or maybe that the deck would give way under me – but at the same time I knew I was safe, really.'

Katie didn't want to risk breaking the sequence of remembering by speaking, but she couldn't help it. 'Who was with you?' she said.

'Grandma, I suppose,' said Sarah. 'I must have been very small – too young to have been here on my own.'

Or Grandpa, Katie thought, but didn't say. 'And these?' she said aloud, reaching out to touch the nearest of the struts. It was cold, and the rough texture of the barnacles put her teeth on edge.

'The caterpillar legs?' said Sarah. 'I do remember thinking a pier looks like a long-legged caterpillar paddling – daring itself to go further out and swim. But I don't know if I thought that back then, about *this* pier. I may have thought it when I was a bit older and saw some other pier.'

'But the black lines in the dream?' said Katie, unable to wait any longer for realisation to dawn, feeling compelled to nudge it along.

Sarah looked at her blankly.

'They're here, aren't they?' said Katie.

Sarah began shaking her head but Katie, in the grip of a powerful mixture of disappointment and relief, couldn't stop, couldn't let go. 'All these black criss-cross bars . . .' she persisted, 'they're the lines, aren't they? And in the dream your face is wet and you think you can't breathe – you must have been down here, something must have happened. Look! It's obvious, if the tide came in now anyone under here would be trapped . . . you must have almost drowned . . .'

'Oh, Katie,' said Sarah, 'I'm sorry. Is that why you wanted me to hurt my feet on this horrible stony beach? To come and look at this? Why didn't you say so? I could have told you this isn't it.'

'But it *has* to be,' said Katie. 'Everything fits.' She no longer knew what she wanted. The thought of her mother trapped by the sea, beaten against the unyielding metal bars, was horrible. She didn't want it ever to have happened. Yet she had been so certain she'd found the answer, to be told she hadn't was like some kind of rejection.

Sarah put one arm around her shoulders and gave her a brief hug. 'Sorry,' she said. 'No one likes to let go of a pet theory, but honestly – this isn't what I see. Look at them.'

She reached up as Katie had and banged on one of the struts with the flat of her hand. It made a soft, flat sound that was instantly swallowed by the faint hiss and scrape of the slow waves.

'These are solid,' she said, hitting the strut one more time. 'Rigid. Geometrical. The lines in my dream are moving, or I think they are – or anyway they look as though they could. And they're not straight – they're looped – like snakes. Or perhaps ropes.'

'Are you sure?' said Katie, but she already knew the answer.

'I'm certain,' said Sarah. 'It must be very annoying – especially after you did such a great build-up, taking us all up the other end so we'd approach from the best angle.'

'No, *you* chose to go that way first,' said Katie. 'I didn't think of it at all till we turned round and I saw – *thought* I saw – the dream lines.'

'Katie,' said Sarah. 'It *is* only a dream. You're not going to find it in the real world.'

The sodden shadows seemed to press closer. Katie shivered. 'Let's get out from here,' she said, 'it's giving me the creeps.'

They walked out from the shadows of the pier's underworld and slogged up the beach to the prom.

'Oh well,' said Sarah, 'at least it was a short-lived disappointment. Listen, Katie, I really haven't come here to unravel my past. I don't even want to try. I can tell you why I came . . .'

'I know why you came,' said Katie, climbing with some relief up on to the smooth surface of the prom. 'It was so the others could go away.'

'And so you could have a bit of a holiday as well,' said her mother.

'I know that too,' said Katie. She felt slightly indignant. 'I thought you knew I knew that. *I'm* the one who wants to get it sorted out, not you. But I *do* want to and I *do* think it's important.'

'It may not be possible,' said her mother. 'Let's just enjoy the break, OK?' Then they both looked around at the windswept promenade, the semi-derelict pier and the grimly shuttered arcades, and began to laugh.

'We can try!' said Katie.

'Let's give up for today,' said her mother. 'Let's go back to the hotel. We're both getting cold and my feet hurt.'

They were the only people in the hotel dining room for dinner, though Mrs Gregg insisted all the rooms were booked. They were also the only two in the lounge afterwards, which was nice because it meant they had control of the television.

They watched a soap opera, a quiz show, and a detective story and then, at about ten forty-five, Sarah began channel flipping until she found a film.

'This'll go on till about one!' said Katie.

'We're on holiday,' said her mother. 'We can stay up late if we want to.'

OK, Amy, delaying tactics again, Katie thought, straining to keep her eyes open and fixed on the screen.

When, finally, they went to bed, Sarah said casually, 'Sea air makes you sleep well. So they say. I hope they're right.'

Katie knew what she really meant – but she just nodded.

ELEVEN

The screaming snatched Katie from out of a very deep sleep. But even as she struggled awake she was aware how distant it was. In fact it was so distant that she sat up in bed in a panic, convinced her mother had walked in her sleep and was somehow lost outside in the night. But Sarah was safe in the twin bed next to hers, and the scream hadn't woken her.

Glad she'd chosen the bed by the window, Katie pulled the curtain a little way aside and looked out.

Grandma would hate this hotel, she thought. We really are on the edge of everything.

Looking out of the third floor window was almost like looking out from the front of a great liner. The streetlight below illuminated a large circle, with everything beyond lost in darkness, so the visible section of road and promenade below looked like a lower deck, curving around above a prow that was surging forwards into the sea.

The wind had risen and the glow from the nearest light was enough to show that the long, dark rolling waves had white breaking crests.

The wind wasn't blowing steadily, but driving through in gusts. First there was a distant moaning sound, like a far off train. Next there was a stronger whine, and then suddenly the lightly falling rain was slanting sideways and a flurry of litter was tumbling past the rusting Victorian shelters and skittering along the prom. Then the gust died, the rain fell straight again and the litter rested.

It was the intermittent crying of the wind that had sounded like a human voice.

The distant moaning began again, and the next flurry pushed its way across the cliffs and then wailed on over the heaving water, making shallow ridged patterns on the shoulders of the waves.

It seemed to move something in the nearest shelter, too, the one right across from the hotel. The shelter had seats on both sides, but the ones facing inwards towards the hotel were clearly empty. Whatever was in there was on the seaward side, and hard to glimpse through the salt-smeared glass.

Then it moved again – but the wind had dropped and couldn't be responsible. Now Katie saw it was a person, a person who had been sitting down but was now standing. Facing out to sea? Or looking through the glass towards her? She couldn't tell.

Feeling suddenly chilly, she dropped the curtain back in place and lay down, pulling the duvet up around her ears.

Sleep came surprisingly quickly. It seemed her mother had been right about the effects of sea air. Next morning, when she sat up in bed and looked out from behind the curtain in daylight, she wasn't sure whether or not she'd dreamt the scene outside the window in the darkness of the early hours.

The dining room was full for breakfast. There were

two family groups with quite young children. There was a group of four middle-aged women who looked as if they might be teachers, and an elderly couple reading newspapers. The only free table was just inside the door. It was laid for two, so Katie and her mother said 'Good morning' to the room in general and sat down.

Mrs Gregg, taking orders for Continental or Full English, seemed flustered and impatient. She had just reached them, notebook in hand, when the front door of the hotel opened and closed.

Moments later a tall, thin girl of about nineteen appeared in the doorway of the dining room. She paused right beside their table, facing Mrs Gregg. She looked harassed and flustered, and she began at once to unbutton her rain-spattered mac with one hand while scraping tendrils of wet hair off her face with the other.

'Christine!' said Mrs Gregg. She held the notebook out to the girl, ignoring the fact that she didn't have a free hand, and said, 'Just this table – I've done the rest.'

'I'm sorry I'm late,' said Christine.

'Only by about an hour, that's all,' said Mrs Gregg sharply.

The families with the young children were too preoccupied to notice. The elderly couple didn't raise their heads from their newspapers. The four middle-aged women began to talk animatedly to each other to save Christine the embarrassment of an audience. Katie and her mother leant together over the *What's On* listings.

'I was up late,' said Christine, plaintively. 'It isn't easy to get up early when you've been up late.'

71

'And what does that tell you?' said Mrs Gregg, loudly. 'Don't you get it, Christine? No, you don't, do you.'

Christine stared at her in silence.

Katie and her mother looked up from *What's On*. Given the position of their table, it really wasn't possible for them to pretend to be unaware of the scene. The two were so close that a few spots of rainwater from the girl's hair dropped on to the edge of their cloth.

'If you can't wake up early because you've been up late,' said Mrs Gregg, unnecessarily slowly, unnecessarily loudly, 'that means you shouldn't *stay* up late.' She paused. 'Doesn't it?' she persisted. 'Not when I pay you to be in early.'

'I couldn't help it,' said Christine. She sounded tearful but defiant.

But Mrs Gregg was already walking away and the next moment she was outside in the hall, banging about at the reception desk. It sounded as though she was slamming the register open and shut.

'I couldn't help it,' said Christine again. She didn't attempt to follow Mrs Gregg, who was in any case making too much noise to hear her. 'I was up listening half the night.'

She looked at Katie and her mother, as if hoping for some support.

Sarah smiled at her encouragingly. 'Listening to music?' she asked.

Christine looked briefly puzzled – then she shook her head. 'No,' she said, 'just listening.'

TWELVE

'Where's your mother?' said Amy eventually, when she'd heard Katie's detailed description of her false hopes about the pier. 'Can she hear this conversation?'

'No,' said Katie. She was sitting in a large armchair beside a fireplace, which was hidden behind an ornamental copper fire screen with curly feet. A line of Dresden china ladies smirked at her from the mantelpiece. The five other chairs and two small sofas were empty, apart from piles of shiny cushions, looking not unlike giant versions of Sweet Memories. The large television screen looked blankly out from a stand on wheels in a corner of the room. 'I'm in the lounge on my own phone,' she went on. 'Mum's up in our room, calling you lot on the hotel phone.'

'Oh,' came Amy's voice, 'so that's who Ben's talking to. Explains why he's on about his dad forgetting to pack toothpaste. Anyway, tell me – what's it like there? Is she OK? Does she recognise anything?'

'She seems OK, but I don't think she remembers much. Just the smell of the sea and walking on the pier looking down through the gaps. And I have to tell you this is not exactly a fun place. It's really dead. In fact it's *so* dead it's supposed to be haunted. What's it like in Wales?'

'Good,' said Amy briskly. 'Sunny. Nice place. We've

73

found a great ravine walk for tomorrow, sounds really scary—'

'*Sunny?*' said Katie, staring at the rain washing down the windowpanes between the frills and loops and fringed sashes of the curtains. 'Sunny there and chucking it down here? Isn't it meant to be the other way round?'

'Probably. But tell me about the haunting.'

'I don't really know anything.' Katie lowered her voice and swivelled in her seat so that she could watch the closed door of the lounge. 'I found a book called *Ghosts of the South Coast*, but this place isn't in there . . .'

'So it's *not* haunted . . .'

'Wait! Don't rush me. The man in the shop went a bit weird when I asked if there was a ghost here – said something about "memories of the past" . . .'

'You mean as opposed to memories of the future?' said Amy.

'Exactly what I thought! Anyway, he was no help, but he got me thinking. And then – there's a girl who works here at the hotel – quite old – I should think nineteen – and the woman who runs the place was being horrible to her because she was late, so Mum and I started talking to her to kind of . . . I don't know . . .'

'Give moral support?' said Amy. 'Solidarity with the workers?'

'Kind of. So then she said she'd been up late. Listening.'

'What was she listening to?'

'She didn't say, but I think it could have been her I saw in the night over in a shelter by the sea. Anyhow, I asked her if the town is haunted and she said "Yes". Just like that!'

'So who's haunting it?' said Amy eagerly.

Katie kicked her shoes off and drew her feet up under her. 'Come to think of it, she's a bit weird herself. Do you know what I suddenly thought? I thought – what if *she's* the ghost!'

'Seriously?' The word came through so high-pitched with excitement it sounded more like an electronic shriek than a human voice.

'No, of course not *seriously*,' said Katie. That was the trouble, she thought, with trying to keep people in touch when they weren't around. They so often latched on to the wrong things – even Amy. 'She's human all right, she's just a bit – a bit *off*.'

'Can you speak up a bit?' Amy asked impatiently. 'I can hardly hear you.'

'No, I can't,' said Katie, keeping her voice level. 'I don't know where anyone in this place is. There might be someone just outside the door for all I know. I'm not about to start yelling down the phone.'

'OK, OK.'

'Right. *I* said "So who's the ghost?" And you know what *she* said?'

'Go on.'

'*She* said, "Don't be afraid of her – she never leaves the sea." '

Amy blew a long sigh down the phone. 'Who?' she said. 'Who is *her* – who is *she*?'

'I don't know. She didn't say anything else – she was serving breakfasts and she went to another table after she said that. And Mum told me to leave her alone. Mum thinks she's not quite right in the head – not quite balanced. She thinks we saw her when we first got here, standing on the beach, all alone in the rain, as if she was waiting for something.'

'Maybe she was.'

'There was nothing out there.'

'Maybe she was waiting for . . . you know . . . *her*?'

'Who?'

'The ghost!'

'The ghost thing is kind of interesting . . .' said Katie, gazing around the lounge walls and noticing that the pictures were all of local scenes, 'but *this* is the bit I want to talk to you about. Listen. I bought a street map and I've found the road where they lived when Mum was little. But I don't know what to do next.'

'Go to the house,' said Amy simply. 'It's what you're there for.'

'But then what? Knock on the door?'

'Or ring the bell,' said Amy. 'Whichever.'

'And what if someone comes? Amy, what if it isn't him? Or worse – what if it *is* him?'

The second thought was so unnerving she looked around the pictures again to try and keep herself calm. The artist seemed to have used a lot of imagination. Maybe the sun did sometimes shine in this place, but surely never *that* brightly. And an English sky was never *that* blue. And the pier certainly wasn't gleaming white. And that little row of three houses on top of the cliffs was pure invention.

'. . . so you have to confront him,' Amy was saying. 'K, he can't be allowed to get away with stuff like that.'

'Stuff like what? We don't know he did anything wrong.'

'You're as suspicious as I am, you know you are. Anyhow, look at it the other way – OK, say we're wrong to suspect him and he's totally innocent – it's only fair on him we find out, isn't it? Isn't it, Katie?'

'I suppose so.'

'I tell you what you do,' said Amy. 'First you get your mother to that street without telling her why. Then you watch to see how she reacts. After that, you have to play it by ear.'

'I don't want to,' said Katie. 'I'd feel I was tricking her. No, worse than that, *betraying* her. It'd be like leading her into an ambush. She doesn't want to see him, she said so on the train.'

'It's for her own good.'

'But *is* it? We don't really know that. Maybe the dream *will* just go away, like she said. Maybe we should leave her childhood alone. Amy, what if she freaks? What will I do? Will I be able to look after her?'

'She's your mother. You should know her well enough to know she wouldn't freak. Even I know that.'

'But it'd upset her. It'd be a real shock.'

'OK, so what you do is you take her to the street, making out you're just going to the shops or something. Then – if she doesn't seem to remember anything or recognise anything – you warn her just before you ring the doorbell.'

'Maybe,' said Katie doubtfully. 'But suppose *he* doesn't live there any more?'

'Then the only people who are going to freak are the

people who *do* live there. They'll think you're casing the joint or something.'

'I can hear someone coming,' said Katie urgently, struggling to get her feet out from under her. For some reason it seemed very important to get her shoes back on. 'What if I ring on the door and it's the wrong people and they think I'm a villain and call the police?'

The door opened and one of the middle-aged teacher-types came into the room. She smiled at Katie, picked up a newspaper from the long low table in front of the fireplace, and took it away to read in the farthest chair possible.

'They won't call the cops,' Amy was saying. 'All you have to do is say you used to live there and ask if you can go in and see if your posters are still on your bedroom wall or something.'

Katie looked across at the woman with the paper. She appeared to be genuinely reading, not listening. Even so, she lowered her voice. 'Why do I need to go in?' she muttered.

'Just because someone else answers the door, that doesn't necessarily mean *he* isn't in there,' said Amy.

'Well – why do I have to pretend I lived there? Why don't I just say Mum used to live there?'

'Because,' said Amy, 'by that point your mum will have guessed what's going on and she'll be walking away. It's vital you get inside. Then your mum'll follow to make sure you're safe. She'll have to. It's what mothers do.'

THIRTEEN

The rain had stopped. The louring sky had lifted and was pale with the promise of sun later. Light glinted on the sea, which was no longer a dark charcoal but greenish, with pale grey and white streaks and flecks.

Today the pier pavilion wasn't capped with four dull gunmetal domes, but with four silvery shapes that somehow looked lighter in weight as well as in shade. The high tide was covering the threatening forest of struts and cross-braces under a swirling skirt of dancing water.

The dry, hopeful weather had brought people out on to the pier decks, and on to the promenade and the beach as well, and the scene which yesterday had been static and mostly grey was now scattered with movement and colour.

Even the air seemed friendlier and easier to breathe, as though oxygen had moved in to fill the spaces where raindrops had been.

It seemed a shame to be walking away from the sea now that it was so much more appealing than before. Still, they had agreed to look at the shopping centre and find the cinema, so they turned inland along one of the narrow side streets that opened on to the prom.

Katie had the street map with her, but she'd memorised the relevant section so successfully that she didn't need to take it out of her pocket. The road where her grandparents had lived was not exactly between the hotel and the shopping centre, it was a few blocks off to the east, on the fringes of the old town, but it wasn't hard to steer her mother towards it.

It seemed that every street, even the ones that were mainly residential, had at least one intriguing-looking shop. There were tatty small shops, piled with junk; elegant little antique shops with perhaps just one piece of perfectly-polished furniture in the window; shops selling second-hand books; old jewellery; modern gifts; clothes, both new and cast-off. Holding the map in her head, Katie found it easy to draw attention to window displays that led them in the right direction – or that pulled them back on track if they'd drifted off.

'Who needs the shopping centre?' said Sarah, relaxed and unsuspicious.

'I like this area,' said Katie complacently, blanking out the faint sense of unease – or possibly guilt – that was growing at the back of her mind.

The first old man appeared just as they had to walk out in the road to go round a bread van which was parked half on the narrow pavement. He was about to walk around the van from the other direction, but he stopped and gestured cheerily with his walking stick that they should go first. The street was one-way, but cars were moving steadily down it, bonnet to rear bumper, and it was all they could do to get between them and the van, walking in single-file.

'Bloody dangerous, these delivery vans,' he said as they smiled their thanks and sidled past him. 'Shouldn't block the pedestrian right of way.' He rapped on the side of the van with his stick as he took his turn to work his way cautiously past it.

That could be him, Katie thought, as she got back on to the pavement beyond the van. He was about the right age – or was he? – what was the right age? About ten years older than Grandma, judging by the wedding photo, so around seventy, then. Was that old man seventy, or older? Older, she decided, and also too short. Even allowing for the shrinkage of age, he was definitely too short.

The next one was taller and slightly younger, with very thin white hair. He was looking in at the window of a small butcher's shop. Katie, used to prewrapped supermarket meat, was repelled by the bloody chunks on the sloping slabs behind the glass – and even more repelled to see the butcher lean over from behind a line of plastic parsley and pick up a handful of mince which leaked and dripped between his fingers.

'It's all right,' said her mother, following her look, 'he's wearing gloves.'

She walked on without giving the old man a second glance, and Katie felt a weak fluttering sensation in her stomach and legs which had nothing to do with the displays of blood and bone.

The third old man was driving a pavement scooter, impatiently and aggressively, probably as impatiently and aggressively as he had once driven a car. Impossible to judge how tall he was, but he was certainly the right sort of age.

Sarah dodged out of his way into a shop doorway.

Then she looked back at Katie and made a face before she moved out of the doorway and walked on.

He's not real to her, Katie thought. It hasn't occurred to her that the man who just rode her off the pavement might be her father.

All these old men, all out and about. And so many other people out as well. It was the time for it, the time of day when holidaymakers and the retired set out, after a late breakfast, to shop or just to look around.

She had pictured him opening the door to them – a blurry figure, possibly with a shockingly obvious family likeness to Sarah, or perhaps to herself. She had even pictured someone else opening the door, someone who couldn't be him, didn't know him, had only lived there for a very few years. The single thing she hadn't pictured was everybody being out, no one at all opening the door, the door remaining shut no matter how often she rang the bell or rapped with the knocker.

How many times might they have to go back to find someone at home? How many times would her mother be willing to go back? Most likely none at all, not one. And what then?

Negative thinking, she imagined Amy saying. Negative thinking, K, keep going – he may be home, there may even be such a strong family likeness that *he'll* recognise *her* and you won't have to say or do anything, it'll all just happen.

Distracted, she realised she'd lost track of the street they were in. The first of the old men had taken her mind away from the map in her head. On the pretence of having a second look at something in a shop window, she ran back to the last corner and read the street name on the wall beside the shop door.

'What were you after?' said her mother, frowning slightly, as she ran back again.

Katie mumbled something about thinking she'd seen a birthday present for Ben, but it hadn't been suitable after all.

Her mother said something, but she couldn't hear through the fog of anxiety surrounding her, so she just shook her head. They were almost there – the map was sharply in her mind's eye now.

The end of the street they were in formed a T-junction with a wider road that ran east-west, parallel with the promenade way behind them. A network of small streets lay north of it. *The* street – the most important street in the town – was the other side of the big road, a very short way along. All they had to do was walk half a block to the T-junction, cross the wide road at an angle, and they'd be there. The only thing she didn't know was which of the four corners of the street the house was on. There was no doubt it was on a corner, the photograph had shown that clearly. That was why the street name was placed so conveniently right beside the gate. But it didn't matter that she didn't know which corner because the house number was imprinted on her brain. There would be no problem finding it.

Her mother said something else – perhaps she asked why Katie was suddenly walking so fast – but Katie couldn't make out the words, didn't bother to respond.

So near, she thought, so very near – just got to get her there, got to get her there—

What she saw when she reached the T-junction was such a shock that she stopped suddenly. Her mother, walking close behind, almost collided with her.

The entire network of small streets to the north of the wide east-west road had gone. In their place stood a huge supermarket and several four-storey blocks of modern flats.

Whether he was at home or out was suddenly irrelevant — the house Sarah had lived in for the first four years of her life simply didn't exist any more.

FOURTEEN

'What have they done?' said Katie. 'It's all gone! It's all new!' She could feel tears of frustration rising in her eyes and she blinked several times to stop them running down her face.

Then, too late, she realised what she'd said, realised that her mother was standing quite still, her hands pushed into the pockets of her jacket, looking at her.

Katie turned to face her. Sarah's expression was coldly angry. 'What was it?' she said. 'What did you think was there?'

Katie shook her head. She didn't know what to say so she didn't say anything.

'You thought you were going to find the house, didn't you?' said Sarah. 'Didn't you? Katie, answer me – you did, didn't you?'

'Yes,' said Katie softly.

Her mother turned and walked off, back the way they'd come. Miserably, Katie followed.

She never knew whether her mother walked back rapidly to the small café near the butcher's deliberately, or if she walked fast to burn up her anger and just happened to run out of steam at the café door. Either way, she went inside and Katie followed.

Sarah pointed to a corner table and Katie sat down at

it and waited until she came back from the counter with two cups of tea.

'All right,' said Sarah, opposite her now and speaking very, very quietly. 'What was going on back there? What did you think you were doing?'

'Like you said,' Katie mumbled, 'I thought we were going to find the house.'

'You told me Grandma didn't give you an address.'

'She didn't,' said Katie, and described the two crucial photographs.

'And what were you planning to do? Ring the doorbell and give him *and* me the shock of our lives?'

Katie looked down at her tea. There were tiny patches of brown scum floating on its surface, she noticed. It didn't seem to matter.

The small café was empty, apart from two old women at a window table arguing about something. And us, about to argue about something, Katie thought.

She looked up at her mother. 'I was only trying to help,' she said.

'I know that,' said Sarah. 'Have you got one of those peppermints, I feel a bit sick.'

Silently Katie took the roll of mints out of her pocket and offered it. Sarah took one and ate it fast. 'You have to stop being secretive,' she said. 'You should have told me where you were taking us.'

'You probably wouldn't have come, if I had.'

'Possibly not. But what you did was horrible. I thought we were just hanging out together. I was enjoying it.'

For a moment Katie was tempted to blame Amy. Then

she remembered her own strong feeling that tricking her mother into visiting the house would be a betrayal. Just because Amy was usually right didn't mean she always was, and it had been stupid, she saw now, to go against her own instinct.

'Sorry,' she said quietly.

'Why did you think it was OK to manipulate me? I never did that to you or Ben – not even when you were small. I always told you where we were going – and why – even before either of you were old enough to understand. Because you can never be sure exactly when a child *is* old enough to understand, and that way I was covered.'

'All right,' said Katie, 'well, you know now. And it doesn't matter anyway because they've pulled the whole street down.'

'Katie, I want you to understand *why* you should have told me. It's about respect. Not respect because I'm your mother, but respect because I'm a separate person and because I have a right to a choice – especially about something as important as this.'

Katie nodded.

Sarah waited a moment, then went on, 'What if the area hadn't been regenerated – what if the house had been there, with him in it? Were you going to confront me with him? Suddenly? Without any warning?'

'I thought it might help you remember something – and understand the dream.'

'Did you! And don't you think a shock like that would be really horrible for me – and for him?' She pushed her tea aside. 'I'm not stupid,' she said, 'I know what you think.'

Katie felt a sickening jolt in her stomach. 'What?' she said guardedly.

'You think he grabbed me by my wrists, and shook me and shouted at me when I was little and the injury to my wrist somehow brought the memory back. Well – maybe he did do that, but so what?'

'So – you have nightmares. And that's not fair.'

'Bad dreams. Big deal. Who doesn't have them sometimes?'

'Not like yours! Not *that* bad!'

'And you didn't think at all about what would happen next, did you?'

'How do you mean?'

'Say we had found him? Say we still do? Then what? If he's in trouble – ill, perhaps, or broke – are we going to take him on, or just walk away? What if he wants to know about Grandma? She certainly doesn't want to know about him. What if he wants her address? Do we refuse to give it? Do we say we'll come back and visit again? Do we invite him up to stay with us, to meet Ben as well as you? He does have two grandchildren, you know. Or do we say – OK, we've had a look at you, now get back into the past where you belong.'

'I suppose it could get complicated,' said Katie reluctantly.

'*Very* complicated. If he's nice and you want to see him again, are you going to tell Grandma what you've done? Or are you going to keep quiet, which would be a kind of lie? If he's horrible, do you want to know you have a horrible grandfather? Do I want to know I had a horrible father? If I look at him and suddenly remember he did shout at me when I was little, how am I better off? The dream might stop – but then I'll have the memory in my conscious mind. And suppose childhood memories come back to tell me that he never shouted at me, that he was always kind to me? Then I have to deal with a load of regrets – and some very odd feelings about Grandma.'

'You mean I've been trying to open a can of worms?' said Katie.

'A can of something, definitely. The trouble is, we're not going to know what's in there until it's open, and then it'll be too late. Once it's open, it can never be shut again.'

'Just as well the house is gone, then.'

'Yes,' said Sarah. She leant back in her chair and patted the sugar bowl back and forth across the table between her hands. 'Except that I don't think we can really stop now.'

'But we have stopped,' said Katie, startled.

'It's been odd coming here,' said Sarah. 'I don't remember anything, I really don't – except I think I remember the smell of the sea and looking down through the gaps in the floor of the pier. And the thing is – even though the house is gone, I know *he* might still be here somewhere.'

She paused, and Katie waited.

'Never coming here at all would have been all right,' Sarah went on at last, 'but to come here and not try to find him would feel a bit like running away. . .'

'But all those things you said . . .'

'I know. They're all true – that *is* how I feel – I feel we're on very dodgy ground. But at the same time . . . I'll tell you something – even though I really didn't know where you were trying to take me – he was sort of on my mind. You probably didn't notice, but all morning we've been passing old men of about the right age, and I've kept thinking . . .'

'I know,' said Katie, 'so have I. Especially the one . . .'

'. . . who almost ran me off the pavement on his scooter,' said Sarah.

'I didn't think you'd noticed.'

'Of course I noticed – I had to shelter in a shop doorway!'

'I mean I didn't know you thought it could be . . .'

'Well I did. And I didn't expect to feel like this but I do.' She leant back in her chair and looked at Katie. Her face was sad. 'We can't stop now,' she said.

'But there isn't anything else we can do . . .' said Katie.

'There are lots of things,' said Sarah. 'But one obvious one is to try the phone book. It's not a very common name – there might not be too many of them.'

'Ring up strangers?' said Katie.

Sarah smiled faintly. 'It couldn't be as bad as knocking on their doors,' she said.

FIFTEEN

There were seventeen of them, but only three had the right initial.

They made the calls up in the hotel bedroom. They used Katie's mobile rather than the hotel extension out of some fear of Mrs Gregg listening in at the switchboard – even though it was hard to see why it would matter if she did.

They sat side by side on Katie's bed. They both had lots of pillows piled up behind them to lean on. They were looking at the phone in Katie's hand.

'When we start calling,' said Katie, 'I'll hold it between us so we can both hear.'

Sarah nodded. 'Of course, he may be dead,' she said, 'and then we don't have to think about him any more.'

'But he may not be,' said Katie. 'Who's going to call? Are you?'

'No. They're more likely to listen to a young voice. If they hear me they'll think I want to sell them double-glazing or a new kitchen or something and they'll probably hang up.'

They sat there on the narrow bed, leaning against each other, for long minutes on end, staring at the phone, listening to the rain making soft sounds on the windowpanes.

The door to the next room opened, footsteps crossed

the floor, a cupboard door clicked and then came the faint rattling of wire coat-hangers.

'Not very soundproof, these rooms,' said Sarah quietly.

'Do you think they can hear us?' Katie whispered back.

'Maybe. Katie – I didn't make a noise last night, did I?'

'No.'

After a few moments there were brisk footsteps, a door opened and closed and the footsteps receded down the corridor. 'Must have been changing to go out,' said Sarah. She sighed. 'At least the wind's dropped.'

'Might be sunny tomorrow,' said Katie. 'Or it might not be,' she added.

'You don't have to do this,' said Sarah. 'You really don't. It's just that I'm not willing to – and I thought you wanted to.'

'I think I want to find him,' said Katie, half hearing Amy's words in her memory. 'I just don't want to make the calls.'

'The addresses are in the phone book,' said Sarah. 'We can go back to your Plan A and knock on doors. It's just that I think the phone is a less startling approach – for everyone.'

'Right,' said Katie. 'What's the worst that can happen? Someone's cross and rude to me. I can live with that.' And she dialled the first of the numbers before she had time to change her mind.

'Perhaps none of them will be at home,' said Sarah. Her voice sounded strained, fearful and hopeful at the same time.

'Sunday afternoon?' said Katie. 'In this weather? You'd think they would be . . .' and at that moment the receiver the other end was picked up and a young man's voice said, 'Yes?'

It hadn't occurred to either of them to work out a speech, something short and simple but clear. The man was polite, but he began to sound bored and impatient as Katie stumbled through her request, stuttering a little and repeating herself as she went.

What had really thrown her was hearing the voice of a man who sounded about the same age as her parents. It suddenly struck her that this could be her grandfather's son by a second marriage. This could be her half-uncle; she could have half-cousins – there could even be a large half-family out there who might or might not be happy to be contacted by their London relations.

But as she made herself calm down enough to listen to his replies she understood that her only connection with this man was the phone link. He had the right initial but the wrong first name. His father also had the wrong first name and, what was more, his father had never lived in this town. He had been born and bred in Bradford and was still there. Katie muttered her thank-yous and switched off the phone.

Sarah, sitting too close to see her easily, was leaning back to look at her with concern.

Katie tried to smile. 'Knocking on doors *would* have been worse,' she said.

'This is bad enough,' said Sarah. 'Let's leave it.'

'Can't,' said Katie, already punching in the next numbers. 'Not after the first try.'

The second number was answered by a woman who sounded old and suspicious. She announced fiercely that no one by that name lived at her address now, or ever had lived there. 'The number is in my son-in-law's name,' she said aggressively. 'And my son-in-law and my daughter visit me often so you needn't go thinking I'm all on my own because I'm not. Furthermore, I have an extremely good burglar alarm system fitted to this house. *Not* that there's anything worth taking here, because I can assure you there isn't.'

Katie did her best to reassure her but she remained tetchy and unconvinced. Sarah signalled to her to hang up and, after one final apology, Katie did.

'It'd definitely have been a mistake to knock on her door,' she said. 'She'd probably have had us arrested.'

'She was scared,' said Sarah, 'poor old thing. I hope she's not going to fret about it.'

'You made me hang up – I was still explaining. Maybe her son-in-law . . .'

'Is his son? Maybe, but she was just getting more wound up – she wasn't going to tell us anything. I think we should abandon this.'

'One more to go,' said Katie. 'Then we'll have to.'

By the time the third call was answered, Katie had her speech all ready. 'I'm sorry to bother you,' she said, 'but I'm trying to trace my grandfather. I know he used to live in this town and I think he might still be here. I've been going through the phone book and ringing people with the same name and initial.'

The woman on the other end of the line sounded both kind and sympathetic. She obviously heard the disappointment in Katie's voice when she had to tell her she couldn't help. 'But I've had a thought,' she said. 'Your grandfather would be an elderly gentleman – do you think he might be in sheltered accommodation? I do know there's at least one place like that locally because my aunt has a small flat there. I can give you the warden's telephone number if you like. It might be worth a try.'

Sarah raked through her handbag for her diary, pulled the tiny pencil out of its spine and wrote down the number as the woman repeated it slowly. Her hand seemed steady, but somehow the digits came out shaky and crooked.

As Katie hung up, Sarah passed her the number. 'We can't ring every nursing home, retirement home and sheltered accommodation unit in the area,' she said flatly.

'I know,' said Katie. 'But I have to try this one now I've been given it.'

She was beginning to feel quite relaxed about calling strangers – especially now she had a clear opening statement prepared. So she wasn't at all prepared for what happened next.

'Oh yes,' came the warden's bright, efficient voice. 'Yes, he's one of our residents.'

In a panic, suddenly and unaccountably hoping to be told it wasn't him after all, Katie searched her brain for any known facts. 'My grandfather was an electrician,' she said wildly.

'That's right,' said the warden.

'He used to live at 17 Tyler Street.'

'He did indeed,' said the warden. 'He moved in here

five years ago, a bit earlier than he'd planned because the council put a compulsory purchase order on all the houses in the neighbourhood. It's been redeveloped and there's a big supermarket and some flats there now.'

'I know,' said Katie weakly.

'I'll put you through to him,' said the warden blithely, and the telephone line clicked on to hold.

Katie sat bolt upright on the bed. She felt her hand clench on the telephone until it bit into her palm. Sarah grabbed her other hand and held it tightly.

And then, heads together, ears straining to catch every tiny electronic whimper from Katie's mobile, they heard the unmistakeable sound of an extension ringing – once – twice – and then being picked up and answered.

SIXTEEN

He shifted his chair closer to the shelf and began to re-arrange the shells, very carefully, very gently. They had come to an agreement, he and the woman. He would dust the shelf and the shells himself and she would leave the display untouched. That way it would be safe from her strong, busy, hurried hands. He didn't really dust any of it, of course, but he moved the shells into different positions in the hope she would believe he had.

When he'd finished, he slewed his chair back to its usual place. Then he looked down at the cordless phone, which was still lying in his lap. He'd been dozing when it rang and the words that had come out of it when he had answered had been so odd, so unexpected, that he wasn't entirely sure whether or not he'd dreamt them.

He put the phone back on its base, on the cluttered table beside his chair, and decided that time would tell if the words had been real or imagined.

Either his daughter and, great heavens, *her* daughter, would turn up next day or they wouldn't.

SEVENTEEN

Like many very small hotels, Sea Spray served dinner early. The menu was limited, with little choice, but the food wasn't expensive and Sarah decided they should go for it. After a still day with glimmers of sun the rain had started again and the wind, though light, seemed to be building. The alternative to Sea Spray's Gammon and Pineapple or Chicken Tikka Salad was a wet and windy expedition to find somewhere else to eat. Eating in and then making a dash for the cinema seemed best.

They knew where the cinema was, now, and the shopping centre. They'd found both that afternoon, during a strange lull, after the telephone calls and before the next wave of rain hit. Their 'appointment', if that wasn't too formal a word for it, was for eleven o'clock next morning, and until then time had to be filled and nervous energy burned off. Too unsettled to buy anything, they'd wandered around like shoplifters, touching things on shelves and raking through racks of clothes, and had finally paid for tickets for the evening showing of a science fiction film Ben had said was brilliant.

The two families with small children were the only other people eating in that evening. Both groups were lively and noisy and Sarah and Katie, back at their sedate table for two by the door, felt as though they were marooned in a pool of silence.

'I remember when you and Ben were that age,' said Sarah wistfully.

'Did we behave like feeding time at the zoo?'

'Worse. I never knew how you got any nourishment. The food seemed to go anywhere but in your mouths. I think you must have absorbed it through your skin and hair.'

Christine appeared from the kitchen door carrying two plates of chicken salad, but before she reached them she somehow allowed one of the plates to slant. A few lettuce leaves and two halves of tomato slipped on to the floor and Christine turned and hurried back into the kitchen.

'Looks like we're going to have to absorb ours through the carpet,' said Katie. 'Shall we call Dad and Ben this evening?'

'Yes. We'll have time before we go out. But . . .' Sarah began to fiddle with the little salt and pepper set in the centre of the table '. . . I'd rather we didn't say anything about . . . about making contact. OK?'

'OK.'

Christine came back from the kitchen with the plates, both now with the same amounts of salad beside the orange slices of chicken. She stepped over the little pile of leaves and tomato and set the plates in front of them.

'Thank you,' said Sarah.

'Is everything satisfactory?' said Christine, in a dull voice.

'Yes, fine,' said Sarah. She waited till Christine had retired to the kitchen again, picking up the dropped salad as she went, and then said, 'I think she's supposed to ask that *after* we've tried the food.'

'She's on automatic pilot,' said Katie. 'You can tell. Mum — I won't say anything about . . . I don't know what to call him! Your father? My grandfather? But we will tell them some time, won't we?'

'Of course,' said Sarah, rather curtly. 'But it isn't as if we've seen him yet, and anyway it isn't something we can talk about over the phone, long distance. It's too — too complicated. We should wait till we're home.'

'All right,' said Katie. She pushed at her pieces of chicken with her fork. She wasn't really hungry. She glanced across at Sarah. Sarah was eating, but without much enthusiasm.

She wondered if Sarah had the same strange feelings in her stomach, but didn't like to ask. It struck her that she felt as if she had some cold, sharp-edged, hollow thing inside her. It felt almost like a huge shell, a bivalve, tightly closed — and going to meet 'him' tomorrow would be like opening that shell and finding out what had been shut away in its hollow centre.

She couldn't think where such an image had come from. And anyway, how could a shell hold so much — all the past, all the fear, all the screaming?

There was a clatter as Christine, clearing one of the tables on the other side of the room, managed to drop several pieces of cutlery at the same time. Mrs Gregg appeared briefly in the dining room doorway and shot Christine a glance of extraordinary malice before withdrawing again.

'She's in a real state,' said Katie quietly. Thinking – a bit like us.

'Shall we ask her to come with us this evening?' said Sarah. 'I'm sure we could get another ticket.'

'If you want,' said Katie, surprised.

'I'm sure Mrs G's going to give her a bad time later on.'

But a little while later, as she cleared away their pudding plates, Christine listened to the invitation, gave a faint smile and shook her head. 'Thanks,' she said, 'but there's something I have to do.'

Later still, as they came down the stairs in their jackets, discussing whether or not there was any point in taking umbrellas with the wind building up the way it was, they glimpsed Christine again. She was hurrying out of the front door of the hotel, her mac tightly belted, collar turned up, shoulders hunched.

Mrs Gregg emerged through her private door behind the small reception desk just after the door closed. Clearly she thought someone was coming in.

'Oh, only Christine leaving,' she said rather sourly, more or less to herself. Then she smiled at Sarah and Katie and said, 'Going out for the evening?'

'To the cinema,' said Sarah. 'What time do you lock the door?'

'Not until you're safely in,' said Mrs Gregg. 'I think you should be back by ten forty-five or so. Enjoy the film.'

They were almost at the front door when Sarah turned back. 'Is Christine all right?' she said. 'She seems . . . agitated.'

'Oh, don't you worry about her,' said Mrs Gregg. 'She's obsessed with the haunting, that's her trouble.'

'There *is* a ghost here, then?' said Katie, in a kind of triumph, thinking back to the man in the shop at the end of the prom and his oblique references to 'memories'.

'So they say,' said Mrs Gregg. 'We've had ghost hunters staying in this very hotel, but of course they never found anything. Nowhere to set up their electronic equipment, you see. It's not as if the haunting's in a building – or on land at all, come to that. One lot even went out in a boat in terrible weather – because of course it only happens in bad weather. Madness! I thought they'd end up as ghosts themselves, but they made it back to shore all right.' She gave a small, dismissive snort. 'Without any evidence, naturally.'

Sarah caught Katie's eye. 'Don't want to miss the beginning of the film . . .' she said.

But Katie wouldn't be deflected. 'What *is* the haunting?' she said impatiently, having listened attentively in the mistaken belief that Mrs Gregg was going to describe it. 'Who's the ghost?'

Sarah edged closer to the front door and grasped the handle.

'Oh,' said Mrs Gregg, shrugging slightly to make the point that she herself gave no credence to such things. 'People think they hear a child crying in the wind on stormy nights around this time of year. They seem to think they hear it on the sea just out there, for some reason. But wind's like that. It often sounds like somebody crying.'

'What child?' Katie persisted.

'There was a local tragedy,' said Mrs Gregg, 'long before I was in this town. You can find out about it at the Lifeboat Museum if you're interested.' She sighed. 'You might think it'd be good for business, but if you run a seaside hotel in England you hardly want to talk about stormy weather in your brochures. It's all too easy for people to go abroad these days.'

Sarah had the front door open now. It seemed she wanted to leave, but couldn't quite let go of something. 'But you think it worries Christine?' she said.

'Oh yes, it's why she came back. She was born here but her family moved along the coast when she was quite young. She came back this winter just gone.' She shook her head disapprovingly. 'The gullible are always with us. And Christine is certainly one of them. She's a bit of a liability, in actual fact. She's moody and unreliable. But in the end I suppose it's more of a nuisance to find someone new than put up with what I've got.'

They didn't speak until they were at the top of the steps and the hotel door was closed behind them. Then Sarah said, 'Nil points for loyalty to her staff. Poor girl. There's something really lost about her, don't you think?'

Katie just nodded. Somehow, out here in the fading light, so close to the whispering sea, she didn't want to mention the voice she'd heard on the wind the night before. Nor did she want to say anything about the figure she'd glimpsed in the shelter – even though, now, she was as sure as she could be that it had been Christine.

EIGHTEEN

There were several ways of getting from Sea Spray Hotel to the sheltered housing block. Out of all of them, the least attractive was to walk the length of the promenade, shunted along by a brisk wind, beside a sullen-looking sea, and then turn left and walk north for a dozen blocks. Because that route formed a huge L-shape, it was also the longest. Nevertheless, it was the way they chose. Unable to stand hanging around in the hotel half the morning, trying to have a conversation about a film neither of them had been able to concentrate on, they'd set out too early. Time had to be used up somehow.

At first they didn't cross the road to the prom but kept close to the small hotels and run-down arcades.

Half a block on, Katie ducked into a shop selling boxes studded with Periwinkles and Necklace shells, chocolates in the shape of Whelk and Clamshells, and plastic jewellery in the shapes of shells unknown. She had noticed that it also sold conventional tubes and packs of mints, toffees and fruit jellies. As she reached for a roll of mints, she spotted a modest display of Sweet Memories at one end of the counter. Looking over her shoulder she saw that Sarah, just behind her, had seen them too.

'Want some?' said Katie, handing her money across the counter to a tired-looking grey-haired woman whose spectacle frames were held together with Elastoplast.

Sarah gave a deliberately exaggerated shudder and wandered outside to wait on the pavement. 'I don't know what it is about them,' she said, as Katie joined her. 'Perhaps I ate too many when I was a child and made myself sick.'

She accepted a mint and looked at her watch. 'Still too early,' she said.

'Look over there,' said Katie, pointing to the lifeboat shed. Its door was propped wide, showing a rectangle of yellow light that looked almost festive against the slate coloured sea and sky. 'The museum's open!'

'I suppose we might as well go in,' said Sarah. She glanced at her watch again. 'And it'll kill a few minutes,' she added.

'Shush,' said Katie, as they crossed the road. 'Don't let the lifeboat hear you insult it.'

There was no lifeboat inside the long wooden boathouse, though. The space where it had once stood was taken up with a series of trestle tables. On the tables lay samples of rope and knots, three styles of lifejacket, two lifebelts and four different model lifeboats. There were also numerous black and white photographs and newspaper cuttings, all in black picture frames. Each exhibit had a neat hand-printed caption propped beside it.

More photographs and newspaper cuttings were framed and hanging on the walls, and a whole collection of them was grouped on a display screen to one side.

At the far end of the shed a man sat at a folding table

reading a newspaper. He was grey-bearded, about sixty, wearing worn blue jeans and a thick navy sweater. Behind him, firmly closed, were the huge floor-to-ceiling doors that opened on to the ramp down to the sea. On the small table in front of him was the familiar boat-shape of a RNLI collection box.

In the corner to his left a girl was standing by a metal filing cabinet, which had a primus stove balanced on top of it, making tea. As she turned round, a mug in each hand, they saw it was Christine.

They hesitated in the doorway. This wasn't the kind of large, impersonal, crowded museum they were used to. It looked as if someone had accidentally left the door open on his private collection and it would be an intrusion to walk in and look at things.

'Christine!' Sarah whispered. 'I'm beginning to feel a bit haunted by Christine.'

Sensing someone in the doorway, the bearded man looked up from his paper and called out, 'Come in! Look around! No charge.'

Christine smiled across at them and carried the tea over to his table. As she put his mug in front of him they heard her say quietly, 'I've left some sandwiches by the stove. You will eat them later, won't you?'

The overhead lights were on but there was no heating and the air felt chilly and damp. Christine hadn't taken off her mac, and she stood beside the man, half leaning on his shoulder, as she drank her own tea. She seemed more relaxed and composed than she had been under Mrs Gregg's eye in Sea Spray Hotel.

Katie and Sarah went across to the long trestle tables

and began, rather self-consciously, to inspect the displays.

'No lifeboat?' said Sarah, unable to think of any other comment.

'Not any more,' said the man. 'It was taken away when it was decommissioned and the RNLI sold up to the council. But that model,' he stood up and leant across the table to point, 'the one nearest you, that's a model of the one that used to put out from here.'

'Why not any more?' said Sarah and she and Katie stood, shoulder-to-shoulder, staring rather blankly at the beautifully-crafted model boat.

'Fishing boats don't go out now. And there's a station just down the coast and the Air Sea Rescue helicopter. Any number of reasons.'

Sarah was looking at a series of black and white prints showing lifeboat crews. The groups varied but one man always seemed to be in the centre. Sarah looked from the photos to the man behind the table. 'Is this you – in these pictures?' she said.

But the man shook his head. 'That's my father. I never went out . . .' he said. He looked as though he might say more, but Christine cut in. 'He made all those models,' she said, with an almost motherly pride. 'All to scale, all perfect.'

'They're great,' said Katie, conscious that she was staring at them uncomprehendingly – her mind filled with thoughts of the old man who was waiting for them, somewhere deep in the town. She knew if she could make herself pay attention to what she was looking at, she'd be able to come up with some intelligent questions. But she couldn't, and even Sarah seemed to have run out of steam. She glanced at her watch for the third time and said, apologetically, 'We can't stay long, we've got an appointment – I think we'll have to come back some time to look at all this properly.'

'As you like,' said the man. 'But I only open when I can. Got a living to earn.'

'This isn't his proper job,' said Christine, as though he needed defending. 'He's really a carpenter. He does this in his spare time, out of respect for those who drowned . . . and the people who tried to save them.'

Sarah had left the tables and wandered over to the display screen. Katie looked at her own watch. She was growing steadily more nervous, suddenly unable to calculate how long the walk to the sheltered housing block would take from here. She looked across at Sarah, standing right in front of the tall, metal-framed screen. The only thing on it she could make out was the heading, in large letters, clearly visible above her mother's head – 'Local Tragedy'.

Sarah was standing quite still, with her back to the room – yet the sense of shock that came from her at that moment was electric. She hadn't moved, and certainly she hadn't spoken, but Katie could sense that something had had a profound effect on her. She scooted round the tables and stood beside her.

The photographs were dramatic and terrible. There was the cliff-top at the end of the promenade, clearly recognisable, but different. A small row of cottages stood a garden's length from its edge and there were signs of immense erosion undercutting it. There was the same scene in darkness and storm, the sea lashing at the cliff-face. And there, horrifyingly, was the cliff giving way, in massive sections – dropping, dropping, dropping, into the teeth of the waves, taking all the cottages with it.

The violent images collided with the tension crackling through the two of them and intensified it powerfully.

Newspaper reports were stuck all around. The columns of small, close type looked too dense to read, but the captions and headlines told the story: the houses gone – the lifeboat launched at great risk to the crew – three men, a woman and a child saved – another child lost.

And there were yet more photographs; the lifeboat being dragged down the ramp by urgent figures, strangely lit, presumably by moonlight; then the lifeboat ploughing through an angry sea, seeming to climb a great shining black wall of water; a man being hauled on board; a child struggling in the water.

'What is it?' Katie whispered, catching hold of Sarah's arm. 'Are you OK?'

'Yes,' said Sarah, her hand over her mouth, her voice slightly muffled. 'It just gave me an awful jolt, suddenly seeing this.'

'A memory jolt?'

'I don't know. No – probably not. *Anyone* would get a shock, wouldn't they? Looking at this? What a *terrible* thing . . .'

Katie's eyes were fixed on the photograph of the child in the water, a little girl of about three, her eyes wide, her mouth open, screaming . . . screaming . . . screaming . . .

'Mum,' she said, pulling urgently at Sarah's arm, rocking her slightly, 'look at her! – Look! Do you think . . .?'

As she spoke she was aware of someone moving up behind them, and the next moment Christine was leaning past Sarah to point at the picture of the terrified little girl. 'That child,' she said, softly, 'that's me.'

Sarah turned to her at once, with obvious relief. Katie half heard her enthusing about what a wonderful organisation the RNLI is, and was half-aware that Sarah was digging around in her bag to find a donation – but most of her attention was on the 'Local Tragedy' exhibit, scanning the reports for more detail.

There was hardly any time, though, because by then it was clear to both of them that they must leave at once or risk being late. They said their goodbyes and set off at a brisk pace.

'You know,' said Sarah, swinging along, one hand holding her hair to try to stop the wind whipping it across her face, 'I really feel I understand Christine better, now we know she went through something like that when she was a tiny child.'

'How much did you read?' said Katie, keeping pace, their speed and the wind in her face making her slightly breathless.

'Only a little. But the awful thing is, they couldn't save everyone. One of the children was lost. I think that may be why Christine seems a bit strange. And why she spends so much time staring out to sea and imagining a ghost child crying. I think it's because she was saved and she feels guilty about the child who wasn't, even though it wasn't her fault. That can happen – survivors feeling guilty – I've heard about it.'

'You didn't read the date, did you?' said Katie.

'What?'

'The accident – the Local Tragedy – it happened in 1950. Before you were born. Definitely before Christine was born.'

Sarah stopped abruptly. They were almost at the end of the promenade – time to turn left up into the town. The jagged cliff loomed ahead. Easy now to understand the warning notices, the great piles of rocks as big as small islands on the beach, the fencing that kept walkers far back from the new, but doubtless still unstable, edge.

'So what did she mean?' said Sarah. 'Why did she say that little girl was her? That's strange.'

'Stranger than strange,' said Katie. 'They saved three men, a woman and a ten-year-old boy. It was that little girl who drowned.'

NINETEEN

He sat in a straight-backed chair, beside the place where a mantelpiece and grate would have been, had the flat been built with such a thing. Instead there was a narrow table with the telephone, two books and a mug on it. The heat came from a radiator behind him.

He had opened the door so swiftly in response to Katie's brief ring on the bell that she wondered if he'd been waiting behind it. He had turned away at once and walked back to his sitting room and his chair, leaving them to follow.

He was stooped and thin, much older and frailer than Katie had expected, and he regained his chair with obvious relief. Maybe he really had worn himself out hovering behind the door, Katie thought, though she had rung the bell at exactly the agreed time. Maybe he was ill. Impossible to guess; impossible to ask.

Katie and Sarah sat side by side on a small settee facing him. Katie noticed a line of seashells on the radiator shelf behind him, and was reminded of her image of a closed bivalve, waiting to be opened to reveal – what?

Just as with the first two telephone calls, she had no prepared speech, no idea how to begin. What exactly was it she wanted to accuse him of? And, if he was guilty, would he admit it? And, more important, was Sarah ready to hear it?

Katie knew she was staring at him. People's faces were supposed to show their true characters when they were old. Did his? Not that she could tell. Did he look like the man in the wedding photo? Yes, but older, thinner – sad.

Just before the silence in the room became too heavy, he looked intently at Sarah and said, 'I know why you're here.'

To Katie it was as unexpected and shocking as if he'd hit her. Was this it? Was he going to make an instant confession of something appalling? She felt sick and slightly dizzy. Out of the corner of her eye she could see her mother, sitting beside her, her hands on her knees, one curled into a fist and the other clasped over it. It looked almost as though she was holding her own hand.

'There's only one reason you'd find me, after all this time,' he said. The skin on his face and hands looked as thin as tissue paper, stretched taut over his bones. 'She's died, hasn't she,' he went on, looking away now, looking beyond them and into the past. 'Men usually go first – and I was sixteen years older, so you would have thought . . . but perhaps it was an accident, or maybe cancer. I've always thought women were more prone to cancer than us.'

Katie shifted uncomfortably, but he wasn't asking, wasn't waiting for a response from either of them.

'I know it feels odd to be an orphan, even when you're grown up,' he went on, 'so I can understand you wanting to check if at least one of us was still here. Well, I am.' He sighed. 'Much good it'll do you to find me – much good I ever was to you.'

His eyes were fixed on Sarah again. Katie wondered what she would say, but he didn't give her a chance.

'At first I thought I'd dreamt the phone call,' he said, 'and then the warden mentioned you and I knew it was real. So then, of course, I thought you must have come about the money.' He gave a short laugh, which had no humour in it at all. 'That shows you how guilty I've felt all these years,' he said, 'because it *couldn't* have been about the money. You never knew about it, and neither did your mother, and anyway it was such a small sum, not worth a journey. Where have you travelled from? Where do you live?'

'London,' said Katie, since Sarah didn't seem able to answer. He gazed into the distance again and began on a long tale of how he had first met his wife, how he had never been worthy of her, hadn't been surprised when she had left, hadn't contested the divorce because he could quite understand she'd want to find someone else. He didn't ask if she had married again – in fact he asked almost nothing at all.

'I look at you,' he said at last, gazing at Sarah in a detached way, as if she was a photograph rather than a person, 'and I can't see the child I knew. But I suppose she's in there somewhere.'

Katie sat forward. Childhood had been touched on – someone had to say something. 'Mum doesn't remember the time she lived down here,' she offered.

He barely looked at her. He was still studying Sarah. 'Do you remember *me*?' he said.

Sarah shook her head. She hadn't moved, but somehow it seemed she'd sunk further back into the sofa.

He sighed. 'Just as well, I daresay,' he said.

Katie's heart hammered in her chest. Here it comes, she thought, stories of things best forgotten. He looked down at his hands and she followed his look. They were thin and weak now, but they wouldn't always have been like that.

But then he held his thin hands out in front of him and said, 'Only a bit of a tremor now, and that's probably age. But when I was drinking . . .' He dropped his hands back into his lap. 'Not any more, though,' he said. 'Not for a long time. Sarah? Sometimes I took you on the beach and you found shells. Sometimes you gave them to me. Do you remember that?'

Sarah looked over at the line of shells on the shelf behind him. Still she didn't speak.

After a moment he shook his head. 'No,' he said flatly. 'You don't. Oh, well, you were very small and I expect a lot's happened since.'

'I've seen photos of you with shells,' said Katie softly, to Sarah.

He heard.

'Yes, I took photos,' he said. 'I've got them all somewhere.' He looked vaguely around the room.

'There's one of her on a miniature lifeboat,' said Katie, conscious she was talking as if her mother wasn't there but not knowing how to avoid it. 'Outside the Lifeboat Museum.' All she could think of to do was push at the memories of that time in the hope – or fear – that he would say something, or her mother would remember something, something somewhere would click.

He nodded. 'That was a ride. Coin in the slot thing.'

115

Katie felt the slight movement beside her as Sarah sat up straight, took a breath, and spoke. 'We went to the Lifeboat Museum on the way here,' she said. Her voice was bright and clear, the voice of someone making polite conversation with a stranger.

He looked quickly from one to the other of them, suddenly more alert. 'So you saw the pictures,' he said eagerly. 'Of the Tragedy?'

'Yes,' said Sarah. 'What a terrible thing.'

'But the pictures are good, aren't they?' he said, his eyes brighter than before. 'Very clear.'

'Did you take them?' said Katie, thinking she understood his sudden excitement.

But he shook his head. 'No, no, not me. Those are professional, I only ever took snaps.'

'Were you here when it happened?' asked Sarah, still sounding bright and over-polite.

She's become Ms Interviewer, Katie thought.

He looked faintly puzzled, as if he'd forgotten what they were talking about. 'Oh – yes,' he said. 'I was a young man then, not yet married. It was a nasty storm but not the worst we've had. Worst result, though, you could say.'

'You'd think they'd have known the cliff was unsafe,' said Sarah. 'You'd think they'd have evacuated the houses.'

'Oh, they did. They'd cleared them a couple of weeks before, when the first deep cracks showed.'

'But the people who had to be rescued? The child who drowned?'

'They weren't from the houses!' he said. He spoke

116

impatiently as if he thought they were being deliberately dense. 'They were sightseers. Locals. Went on the slipway to watch. The cliff – the houses – all went at once. Set up a massive wave and some of them were dragged under – including the child.'

Then the faraway look returned, as though he was seeing beyond the room and its occupants and into another time. 'Bill Craigie never got over it,' he said.

'Who?' said Katie.

'Bill Craigie. Skipper of the lifeboat. The others were saved but he couldn't save her. She was so small – he said she just slipped away.' He gave another of his short, humourless laughs. 'Couldn't save her, but he saved me,' he added.

'Saved you from drowning?' said Sarah, startled into using her normal voice.

'No! I wasn't down there! I didn't know anything about it till next day. No – the thing was – Bill Craigie took to drink in a big way after he lost that child. Blamed himself, though it wasn't his fault – he'd done his best. Drank himself to death. Took him a good few years, but he did it. He died not long after you and your mother left. Gave me a shock, him dying of drink. Pulled me up. Make me stop myself. So – he couldn't save her, but he saved me. Doubt if that'd have been much consolation if he'd known. You were lucky to get in to the exhibition – John doesn't open often, just when he can.'

'Was John here when it happened?' said Sarah, back to making polite conversation.

He frowned at her. 'Well of course he was!' he said.

117

'John Craigie is Bill Craigie's son, isn't he? Looks exactly like him.'

'We don't know anything about this place,' Katie snapped, suddenly irritated with him. 'You can't expect us to know that kind of stuff.'

He looked away, lowering his head slightly, avoiding confrontation. When he looked back his face was flushed and his eyes more watery than before. 'I didn't just do it for the money,' he said, rather plaintively. 'It was interesting. Exciting.'

'So you *were* down there?' said Katie.

'No, no, not *then*. I wasn't there then.'

'Well, what is this money you keep on about?'

'It seemed a lot, then,' he said. He was still flushed and all at once his veins seemed very visible – knotted blue in his hands, bulging and throbbing in his temples.

'I think we'd better leave this,' said Sarah softly.

'Do you know about the haunting?' said Katie, not really knowing if she was changing the subject or not – not really knowing what the subject had been.

He sighed and brushed at the back of each of his hands with the other, as if soothing the straining veins. 'Depends what you mean by haunting,' he said. 'Depends if you're talking about being haunted by spirits from another world, or haunted by guilt and regrets from this world.'

A sudden squall rattled the window and something outside in the street blew over with a clatter.

Sarah stood up. 'We should go,' she said firmly. 'We should get back to the hotel before the weather gets worse.'

118

He clamped his hands on the arms of his chair and heaved himself into a standing position. 'I expect you're right,' he said and led the way, slowly, to his front door.

As they stood together in the corridor outside his flat, looking back at the thin figure outlined in the narrowing opening of the door, Katie heard herself say, 'We'll come again. Can we come again?'

'If you like,' he said, and closed the door gently.

'Why did you have to say that?' Sarah asked, striding towards the street door. 'That was a gruesome half hour. He doesn't *seem* like my father – I haven't *got* a father – I never had a father. It was only all right when I let myself think of him as a complete stranger – which he *is*. And we didn't get anywhere and we never will. He's muddled and if you push him he gets all worked up. It was pointless and horrible. Why did you say we'd go back?'

'He knows something about the accident,' said Katie, hauling the street door open and letting a swirl of wind and litter into the narrow hall. 'The accident – the Tragedy – has to be relevant – but I couldn't follow him. He didn't explain properly.'

'He's confused,' said Sarah. 'He can't explain. There's no point coming back.'

'Mum, I'm sorry,' said Katie, 'but I *really* want us to. It isn't over yet – I know it isn't.'

TWENTY

They walked back to the hotel along side streets, avoiding the sea front for as long as possible. The wind was less noticeable amongst the sheltering rows of buildings, but it attacked at street corners with surprising force.

Although they were such a short way inland, the sounds the wind made back here were different. In fact, away from the beach, it didn't seem to have its own voice at all. The sounds were actually made by other things – a gate slamming; an empty plastic bag flapping along the pavement like a grounded bat until it wrapped itself around the stem of a lamppost; the sign suspended above the jeweller's swinging creakily to and fro.

At first they walked in silence, each too preoccupied with her own thoughts to say anything.

Katie longed to telephone Amy. Amy would be sure to come up with some ideas, some suggestions for the next move.

Sarah was frowning to herself, her chin tucked down into the collar of her jacket. After a while she said, 'I should have told him she's still alive.'

'He didn't give us a chance,' said Katie.

'I know, but I should have interrupted and told him.'

'It's better like this,' said Katie. 'Now he won't ask for

her address or phone number – and we won't have to tell her we saw him.'

'But it felt wrong,' said Sarah. 'It felt as though I was denying her.'

'You weren't denying her anything,' said Katie, misunderstanding. 'She doesn't want to know about him.'

'No – I mean it felt as though I was denying she exists – letting him think she's dead, when really she's up there in London, at an art class, or shopping or listening to the radio or something.'

'She'd rather you did that than told him and he rang her up,' said Katie. 'I bet you.'

'I'm *so* closely related to him,' said Sarah, ignoring her, 'but I feel no connection to him at all. I looked and looked at him and I just saw a stranger. An old man just like any old man. It was like looking at those old men on the way there this morning and thinking, Could that be him? – But even though I know this one *is* him, he doesn't seem any more important than any of the others. It's such a strange feeling.'

'I've been thinking . . .' Katie said, '. . . you know that picture of the child in the sea? When I first saw it I thought it might be you – I thought you might have almost drowned and that's what you were dreaming about. But it wasn't you because that child did drown, and anyway it happened before you were born . . . but maybe someone told you the story about her drowning when you were very small? Could that be it?'

Sarah didn't answer at once; she walked steadily on, looking at the pavement, only glancing up briefly from time to time. At last she said, 'It's possible. I don't remember that story. But I can't get the pictures out of my head – there's something about the pictures, something odd.' She shook her head. 'I can't get hold of it,' she said.

'He was really keen on those pictures,' said Katie. 'Do you think he's one of those people who like looking at accidents?'

'I don't want to think about him just now,' said Sarah. 'Everything's jumping around in my head – I need to let it settle.'

They crossed the wide street that ran past the shopping centre and right on down to a distant grey sea at the far end, a sea that appeared to stand higher than the land, bulging between beach and horizon.

The wind wrapped their hair around their faces and flapped the edges of their jackets. Here, where it had a clear run up the street, it found a voice – an intermittent, wailing voice.

'Does it sound like a child crying to you?' said Katie, uncertainly.

'Kind of,' said Sarah, hurrying for the opposite pavement and the shelter of the next street. 'But wind often sounds like that. Doesn't it?'

What would Amy say? Amy would see it from some different angle. She'd come up with something unexpected, even shocking, like her idea that Sarah had – perhaps – been abused by her father as a tiny child. She would make a connection between little Sarah in the dream, frightened, screaming, wet, unable to breathe properly and the little girl in the sea, frightened, screaming, wet, unable to breathe properly, who had drowned ten years before Sarah was born – because after all there *had* to be a connection.

Reincarnation!

No, Amy, no. We've talked about that and we agreed that we don't know if we believe it or not, but that if it does happen you wouldn't be able to remember anything at all from your previous life or lives.

We can't be sure about that.

Amy, you know perfectly well that memory is stored chemically in the brain, and if a person is dead the brain doesn't function any more.

But if there is such a thing as reincarnation, something must be carried over.

Yes, the spirit. And the spirit would find another body, and take with it any spiritual qualities it had earned on earth – good ones or bad ones. But that's all, no memories.

Don't you think it might remember how it died?

No, Amy, because the spirit doesn't die, only the body. The spirit wouldn't remember events that affected a previous body – it wouldn't need to.

'You're whispering to yourself,' said Sarah.

'I was thinking something through,' said Katie. She added (though not aloud), I was having an argument with Amy, which was a bit unfair on her because I was doing both sides.

But even though the absent Amy had lost the argument, Katie found it hard to let it go. There had to be a connection – might it be reincarnation, after all? Might it really be that? And then there was Christine's claim. Where did she fit in? It seemed wise to approach the subject cautiously.

'Do you think,' she said experimentally, 'Christine believes she's a reincarnation of the little girl who died?'

'Those pictures . . .' Sarah began, giving no indication that she had heard the question. Then she stopped on a blustery corner. 'Is this where we go – down to the hotel?'

'Not sure,' said Katie, hunched against the wind beside her. 'I didn't bring the map.'

'We'll have to try it,' said Sarah.

It wasn't raining yet, although fat clouds were piling up above the sea. Walking down the road towards the promenade, with the sea and the heavy grey sky ahead, felt strange. Katie had a sudden vivid sense of what her grandmother had meant when she had said being at the seaside was like being on the edge of everything. And walking along a street which sloped gently towards the water, watching the waves seem to grow larger as they got closer, made her feel as though they were walking towards an edge which might lure them on and on, and over into oblivion.

'I hope we stop in time,' she said, mostly to herself.

'Those pictures,' said Sarah, again, 'I knew there was something odd about them and I've just worked out what it was. They were too good. They were too clear.'

An image came sharply into Katie's mind, the image of the child in the black water, crying. 'The photographer who took the picture of the little girl – drowning,' she said. 'How could someone *do* that? Why wouldn't you chuck away the camera and try to save her?'

'Think about it,' said Sarah. 'Where was the photographer? Somewhere quite close – but how? In a boat? On that rough sea? If so, why are the pictures so sharp and clear? Why aren't they out of focus? And why can you see those men dragging the lifeboat out so clearly – it would all be a blurry muddle – they wouldn't be silhouetted like that unless there was light behind them. But it was night-time.'

'Moonlight?'

'If the moon was behind them you'd see it in the shot – if it was above, it wouldn't silhouette them like that. Would it? And whoever took the picture of the cliff falling was close, either on the water in a boat or right down at the edge of the sea – so why wasn't he or she swept away by the wave that caught the others?'

'I don't know,' said Katie. 'What do you think, then?'

They reached the end of the road, turned right, and there ahead was the long narrow sign spelling out Sea Spray Hotel, all down the length of the long narrow building.

'I never thought that dreary place would look welcoming,' said Sarah.

They climbed the stone steps, pushed through the door and paused in the empty lobby to get their breath back.

'What about the pictures, then?' said Katie. 'What are you thinking?'

Sarah leant back against the lobby wall, still breathing rapidly from the battle with the wind. Katie hadn't noticed before how pale she was, but her voice was strong. 'I don't think those photos are of the Tragedy at all,' she said.

'What do you mean?'

'They can't be photos of the real thing. I think there must have been a reconstruction.'

'You mean – like police crime shows on TV?'

'Kind of.'

'Why would anyone do that?'

'I don't know. Perhaps someone made a film – or a video – maybe they made it specially for the exhibition. Maybe there's an AV show there and we didn't spot it.'

'But why would they? It'd cost a lot, wouldn't it? Would anyone bother – just for a tiny little museum like that?'

'I don't know – but nothing will convince me those were pictures of the actual event. I think they were stills taken from a film or video reconstructing the original disaster.'

Katie stared at her. Something was beginning to bubble up in the back of her mind.

'And I'll tell you something else,' Sarah went on. 'I think when Christine was three or four years old someone used her to play the part of the child who drowned.' She pushed herself away from the wall. 'Come on, let's get our key,' she said.

Katie felt herself breathing very shallowly – letting the idea grow to full size before she spoke it.

Sarah walked over to the empty desk and leant across it to unhook their room key. 'I think that's what Christine meant,' she went on, 'when she said the child was her. It *was* her. Playing the part. Except she was too

126

young to act – she was *really* frightened.' She gave a slight shudder. 'What a terrible thing to do to a child.'

She turned back, the key in her hand. 'What?' she said. 'Why are you staring at me like that?'

'Or *you*!' said Katie. 'Maybe someone used *you*!'

At that moment Mrs Gregg bounced out of the door behind the reception desk like a jack-in-the-box. 'Oh, you're back,' she said. 'There's been a telephone call for you. An elderly-sounding gentleman – wouldn't give his name – said you'd know. Said he wants you to go back right away. There's something he has to tell you. It sounded urgent.'

TWENTY-ONE

At first Katie thought he'd called them back because he'd been burgled.

The telephone was on the floor. Every drawer in the chest in the corner of the room was hanging so far open it looked as though it could fall at any moment. The doors of the built-in cupboard at the back of the room were open, too, and things had been pulled off the shelves and left heaped on the carpet below. Photographs seemed to be everywhere, in their packets and out of their packets, in unsteady piles or spread out in groups.

He was clearly agitated, and the pink wateriness of his eyes and the slight blurring of his speech suggested he'd had at least one drink to steady himself.

Then she realised that if he had been burgled he'd have called the warden, not them; also that the phone was on the floor to make space on the table for a selection of photographs, neatly arranged.

Not burgled, looking for something. And it seemed he'd found what he was searching for.

'Sit down,' he said, flapping them towards the sofa. 'Sit down.' He settled himself into his own chair, dragged a packet out of his pocket and held it out to Sarah. 'Have one,' he said.

The packet was instantly recognisable. It was transparent and filled with square, pastel-coloured sweets with sharply pointed corners. They rattled softly together with the tremor of his hand. The words Sweet Memories were written across the top of the pack in the familiar curly script.

'Yesterday,' he said, 'as soon as I knew you were coming, I asked the warden to get some for me.' He leant further forward, pushing the open packet closer to Sarah.

Hesitantly, she took a sweet. He swung the packet across to Katie, but she shook her head. He didn't insist, just put it down beside the pictures. He stared fixedly at Sarah.

'They weren't called Sweet Memories in our day,' he said. 'They were called Satin Cushions. I forgot to bring them out last time.'

Katie felt anger surge up inside her. 'Did you call us back here in a panic because you forgot to offer us *sweets*?' she said.

He ignored her. 'They used to be your favourites, Sarah,' he said. 'Do you remember?'

There was a silence which held something indefinable.

'I used to give them to you afterwards,' he said. 'To stop you crying.'

Now the silence held the distant crying of the wind, like an echo of a child screaming, an echo of Sarah screaming.

'After *what*?' said Katie, hardly knowing what she was saying, hardly recognising her own voice. 'What did you do to her?'

She might as well not have spoken. He was only

interested in Sarah, fixing her with his watery gaze. Sarah was staring back at him, sitting completely still, her hand with the sweet in it resting on her lap.

He leant back. 'I want to set things straight,' he said – but before he could go on, the door opened with a suddenness that made them all jump. A middle-aged woman, carrying a plastic box with dusters trailing over its sides, marched in and cast a fierce look over the room.

'The *mess*!' she said. 'What *have* you been up to?'

He sank down in his chair, sulkily, like a child. 'Looking for stuff,' he mumbled.

The woman dumped her duster box and reached around outside the still-open door to drag in a vacuum cleaner. She was so full of energy and determination, her mind obviously set on exactly what she planned to dust or sweep first, that it wasn't until she'd closed the door that she noticed he wasn't alone.

'Oh,' she said, smiling at Katie and Sarah in quite a friendly way. 'You've got company. I didn't realise. Do you want me to come back later?'

Katie, still struggling with the implications of that word 'afterwards', somehow managed to smile back at her, but neither she nor Sarah knew how to answer her and neither, it seemed, did he.

The woman stood there, waiting, clearly expecting to be introduced. When no one spoke, she peered over the back of his chair at the neat piles of photos on the table beside him and nodded understandingly.

'Oh, he's telling you all about the Tragedy, is he?' she said, as if he wasn't there. 'I'll come back and clean up later. You're the first visitors he's had, I won't interrupt you.' She glanced around the chaos on the floor and gave a short laugh. 'Anyway, I can't sweep with all that lot on the carpet and he doesn't like me moving things.' She looked down at the slumped figure in the chair. 'You don't, do you?' she prompted.

'No,' he agreed.

She gestured with the duster box at the long narrow shelf where the shells stood, silent and brittle, perfectly spaced. 'I'm not allowed to touch those,' she said. 'Someone special gave them to him.' She looked first at Katie then at Sarah. She didn't say any more, but her expression was plainly asking, Was it you?

Sarah seemed to wake herself out of a trance. 'Everyone here seems to know about the Tragedy,' she said, in her polite 'social' voice. 'What a terrible thing.'

'Oh it was,' said the woman, still as nameless to them as they were to her. 'Of course I was very small when it happened so I only know what I was told, but I know it broke Bill Craigie's heart.' She put the box of dusters down and leant on the vacuum handle. 'You've been to the museum?'

Sarah nodded.

'Then you'll have met his son, John Craigie. Spitting image of his father.'

Katie, sensing available information, forced herself to pay attention. 'And there was a girl at the museum,' she said. 'Christine.'

'That's John Craigie's daughter.'

'Oh she's his *daughter* . . .' said Sarah.

'His sister was Christine, too,' said the woman. 'John and Christine were Bill Craigie's children. John was about ten when it happened. Christine was just three. A lot of people were down by the beach, wrapped up warm and watching. The houses had been cleared, and there were no boats out, but the lifeboat crew were there – just in case. And just as well. They say Bill Craigie's wife was making tea in the lifeboat shed. John was supposed to be keeping an eye on Christine. Then some foolish adults went down the slipway for a better look, and young John went too. No one knows if he took Christine with him, or if she just followed. They say when the cliff and the houses hit the sea the tidal wave was a monster, a real monster. They saved the adults and they saved young John, but Bill Craigie didn't get a good enough grip on the little girl and the sea took her. He dived in after her but he never found her. Her poor little body was washed up days later, way down the coast.

'He never got over it. Nor did John. Years later, when he had a daughter, he wanted her called Christine, after his lost sister. And so she is.'

'That's why Christine . . .' Katie began. Then she stopped, not knowing quite what she wanted to say. Perhaps, That's why Christine stands by the sea, listening.

But the woman finished the sentence in her own way. 'That's why Christine came back,' she nodded. 'Her mother moved away years ago, but Christine came back as soon as she was eighteen. Her father told her she's a reincarnation of his little sister, you see. He wants her to be, because that would mean he didn't really cause his sister's death. Not her final death, anyway.'

'But he didn't cause it,' said Sarah. 'It was an accident.'

'Yes, but he thinks he should have prevented it. And his father thought he should have saved her. The *guilt* those two men built up for themselves!'

Abruptly she bent down and picked up the duster box. 'I mustn't run on like this,' she said. 'You want to talk to each other, not me.'

She opened the door and dragged the vacuum cleaner out. 'It's all that guilt that's trapped that poor child's spirit here,' she added. 'Crying all over again any time there's a storm.'

She dumped the cleaning gear outside the door and then leant in briefly to close it. 'You let him show you the pictures from the film,' she said as she did so. 'He likes to show them.'

The film. The words spoken so casually, as if everyone had always known there was a film.

'So the pictures in the exhibition,' said Sarah softly, when she'd gone, '*are* stills from a film.'

He brightened. 'Of course,' he said, eagerly, sitting up straight and beginning to shuffle through the photographs.

'And the child in the picture?' said Katie. 'In the museum? That was my mum? That was Sarah?'

'Of course,' he said again, slightly impatiently this time.

Katie glanced at Sarah, but Sarah was watching him silently, with that extreme stillness, as if she was listening to something she had waited to hear all her life.

'It was made as an exercise by the film school from the university just north of here,' he went on. Enthusiasm clarified his mind. 'They used it to demonstrate their skills

– model-making, lighting, acting, cutting and editing. The model of the cliff, and the scale models of the houses, were all based on old photographs. The lifeboat was real. They borrowed it just after it was decommissioned and just before it was taken away. They *backlit* the shot and *intercut* it with film of the sea in bad weather.'

His eyes were gleaming now, with the pleasure of remembering the few technical terms he'd picked up all that time ago.

'They filmed the rescue scene and the drowning in the swimming baths in town here. They're closed down now. The pool was full-size but people want posh facilities and classy showers these days. They brought in a wind machine, and what with that, and lighting effects, and intercutting with shots of the real sea in a real storm . . . it was very effective.

'I heard they were looking for extras and I went along. They had enough men, but they needed a little girl. You were perfect, Sarah. You were exactly the right age, and very appealing.'

He picked up the batch of photographs and held them out. Sarah got up, put the Satin Cushion back on top of its packet and accepted the pictures. As she sat down, Katie leaned over her shoulder to look.

Some they'd already seen, but there were others – the child screaming in the water; several of a man in an oilskin, leaning dangerously far over the edge of a boat, hauling at the crying child by one arm, his mouth open in a great shout; one of the child slipping away under the water and the man tipping his head back in a howl of grief.

134

Katie was trying to disentangle two conflicting emotions; huge relief because now she understood that he hadn't done the appalling thing Amy had suggested; and rage at the horrible thing he had done. She linked her arm through her mother's and hung on tightly.

'They had good actors at that film school,' he went on. 'The man who played the part of Bill Craigie really made you feel the anguish that man felt when he lost that child.' Suddenly tired, he leant back in his chair and looked sorrowfully at the rejected Satin Pillow.

'Were there black snaking lines in the air?' said Sarah quietly.

He looked briefly puzzled. Then his memory cleared and he nodded. 'Cables,' he said. 'For the lights and so on. You remember those?'

'Was I frightened?' said Sarah.

He chuckled. He was looking more relaxed now. 'You screamed,' he said, 'but you were supposed to. In between takes I gave you your favourite sweets and you soon stopped crying. Then they did another take and made you cry all over again. We got through three whole packets of Satin Pillows.'

'How could you *do* it?' said Katie.

'She was too young to mind,' he said, reassuring himself.

Katie looked at Sarah. Surely she would want to say something, yell at him, throw his horrible shiny sickly sweets in his face. But Sarah was calm and quiet, just watching.

'You're not supposed to terrify little children, just for

fun,' Katie shouted, 'just for a *film*! You shouldn't treat an *animal* like that – but your own *child* . . .'

He blinked at her. 'She was quite safe. They didn't take any risks with her. She was never in any danger.'

'But *she* didn't know that!' said Katie. 'Don't you have any feelings of guilt at all?'

The vague smile left his face and he sat upright, leaning forwards. 'About the money?' he said. 'Oh yes. That's always haunted me.'

'Not about *money*,' said Katie. 'About putting her through that.'

He shook his head dismissively. 'It was only half a day. She forgot it as soon as it was over. It was nothing to her. Children cry all the time.' He looked quickly at Sarah. 'It didn't do you any harm, did it?' he said.

Katie sat still, not breathing, pouring all her energies into willing Sarah to talk about the nightmares. It had to come from her, no one else could tell him – she must, she must, surely she must.

Sarah contemplated the thin, watery-eyed face that was turned towards her, its expression one of sudden acute anxiety.

'You've already told us I was too young to mind,' she said.

The anxiety left his face at once. Katie felt her hands clench. He nodded and pulled a cheque out of the pocket of his cardigan. 'It's for a hundred pounds,' he said. 'They didn't pay me nearly as much as that for you, but I'm trying to allow for inflation and interest.'

'What *did* they pay you?' said Katie savagely. 'Thirty pieces of silver?'

He didn't get it. 'They paid me in notes,' he said vaguely, handing the cheque to Sarah. 'You earned the money. I should have given it to you, or your mother. Please take it – it's weighed on me all these years.'

Sarah leant forward and took it.

'At the time,' he went on, 'I hadn't enough in my pocket to buy a round at the pub – so that meant I couldn't meet my friends. I needed the money. You didn't need it, what would you have spent it on? Satin Cushions, probably, Sweet Memories – and I bought you those anyway.' He prodded the packet rather sadly. 'Don't you like them any more?' He looked at Katie. 'Don't you?'

No one answered him. 'I never told your mother,' he said, turning to Sarah again. 'She never saw the exhibition. She said the sea gave her the creeps. She hated the story of the accident and how everyone kept on about it. She hated the way no one seemed to remember the child alive. They didn't remember her running about and playing, they only remembered how she was lost. They should have let her go. The past belongs in the past. That's why I never tried to find you or your mother – I belonged in your past. And she knew where I lived, but she never got in touch.' He sighed. 'And she never will now, will she?' he said.

'No,' said Katie, firmly and truthfully, 'she never will.'

Later, neither of them could remember leaving.

Walking down the road, leaning into the strengthening wind, Katie said, 'I feel sick. I feel as if I've eaten packs and packs and packs of those horrible sweets.'

'You liked them when you tried them before,' said Sarah mildly.

'That's before I knew him,' said Katie. 'Why aren't you angry? Why didn't you yell at him? Why didn't you tell him that because he was so greedy and so stupid you wake up screaming most nights?'

'Because there's no point loading guilt on to someone. Guilt's destructive.'

'But he *should* feel guilty!'

'Why? What good would it do?'

'When people do bad things they *ought* to feel guilty,' said Katie. 'Guilt stops them doing the bad thing again.'

'But he's never going to do it again anyway,' said Sarah. 'And Bill Craigie is never going to fail to save his little daughter again. And John Craigie is never going to let his little sister get herself into danger again. Guilt's no use to any of them.'

'If I'd known you were going to let him off the hook,' said Katie savagely, 'I'd have had more of a go at him.'

'There's useful guilt and there's destructive guilt,' said Sarah. 'Useful guilt can do what you said – make people behave better. Destructive guilt just hangs around and drags everyone down and spreads misery and achieves nothing. If I dumped that on him then I ought to feel guilty myself. Shall we go back by the seafront?'

'Do you want to?' said Katie, surprised.

'We could see if the museum is still open – ask if they have the film. I'm not sure I want to see it – but I'd like to know if it's possible.'

Katie nodded. She suddenly felt too tired to speak. Sarah, either because she was tired as well, or because she was organising her thoughts, didn't speak either.

By the time they reached the promenade the wind off the sea was so strong it would have been hard to talk anyway. It was now as clamorous as they'd ever heard it. It seemed to have a thousand voices – yet one was somehow separate and different from the rest.

Impossible to guess if it was caused by the shape of the cliffs, or perhaps the arrangement of the buildings; impossible to guess how the wind achieved the effect – but now, without any doubt, it carried the thin, desperate voice of a frightened, crying child.

TWENTY-TWO

It was as they reached the promenade that Sarah and Katie remembered they hadn't eaten lunch. They had walked south along the North Road and arrived at the sea front with the ragged cliffs on their left and the long seafront road, bordered by the promenade, running off to their right. And there, next to the corner shop with the newspapers, maps and beach gear, was the little café.

It was definitely past lunchtime but not yet teatime and the café was deserted.

They hovered by the formica-topped tables and plastic chairs, unsure if it was self-service or not. A woman came out from behind the counter, not smiling, and said briskly, 'It'll have to be something quick, I'm closing up.'

'Oh,' said Sarah, glancing at her watch.

'Not because of the time,' said the woman, 'because of the forecast.'

Then, probably because they looked so forlorn and puzzled, she relented. 'Go on, sit down,' she said. 'What is it you want? It's just that they're forecasting gale force winds for later and I want to close and get the shutters up. I don't want the windows blown in.'

They had beans on toast and tea, which they ate in silence, apart from the complaining voice of the growing storm, which rose and fell outside and sometimes rattled at the door.

Katie's stomach felt empty but her chest felt full of things she wanted to say. It was hard to force the food down past them. Yet neither she nor Sarah wanted to speak in the café. If it had been crowded it would have been different, but the woman behind the counter – shutting things away in the fridge and looking frequently in their direction in the hope they'd finished – would have heard everything. It was too personal, and too peculiar, to be anything but very private.

Katie slid her mobile out of her pocket and on to her lap. She longed to ring Amy, but didn't quite like to in front of Sarah and a stranger. Surreptitiously she switched it on and glanced down at it. Missed call, said the display, followed by Amy's mobile number.

That settled it. 'Just going to the toilet,' said Katie, 'won't be a minute.'

It was a tiny cubicle, not surprising in such a small café, but vacant. Katie pressed redial, and to her relief Amy answered almost at once.

Katie could hear background voices and distant birdsong but she didn't ask Amy where she was, she just said, 'I have to be quick,' and then rattled out the story as fast as she could. 'I'm glad we know what happened,' she finished. 'And I'm *very* glad it wasn't child abuse.'

'But it was,' said Amy simply. The background sounds had receded; she had obviously managed to move away from the family. 'Sexual abuse is only one kind – and it's probably the worst and sickest – but what he did *was* abuse. He bullied her – he terrified her – he put her through *torture* – and all for money!'

Torture. A horrible, rending, tearing word.

'You're right,' said Katie, anger building again. 'That horrible old man – and I don't even know if finding out has helped her.'

'I'm walking behind the others,' said Amy, 'but we're going down into a valley. I could lose the signal. Listen – it *will* have helped. He was big and strong when he bullied her, and she was small. Now he's old and frail and she's stronger than him. That'll do it – trust me.' Her voice was getting fainter and there were gaps in her speech now. 'Have you found out any more about Christine and the haunting?'

Rapidly, Katie gabbled out Christine's story.

'So her father abused her, too,' came Amy's voice, chopped into electronic snippets.

'No, he didn't. What do you mean?'

'Come on!' said Amy. 'Do you really think it's OK to say to your kid, "You're not really my child, you're really my dead sister." '

Even in the small cubicle, with the door shut, Katie could hear the muted sounds of the storm protesting outside.

'Oh,' she said. 'I suppose that could have a weird effect on someone.'

'And it did, didn't it? You said she was odd.'

'I have to get back,' said Katie. 'Mum'll think I've been taken ill in here.'

Amy's response was no more than a faint crackling sound, which then cut out.

Katie switched off and hurried back into the café.

As she reappeared, Sarah got up and carried the plates and cups across to the counter. 'I'm sorry we held you up,' she said. 'Thank you for feeding us.'

'No trouble,' said the woman, smiling, relaxed now they were going. 'But I'll be happy to close. It's wind damage I'm worried about, but I'll be glad to get home inland, away from that wailing child. It really gives me the pip.'

'You hear that too?' said Katie.

'Who doesn't?'

'But it *is* only the wind,' said Sarah.

'I suppose it is. But it never seems to make that noise any other time of year. And once you know the story, you can't hear it as anything else but crying.'

And it was true. Once outside the café the voice in the storm seemed undeniably human – even though all reason said that it couldn't be. It wasn't there all the time – it was intermittent – sighing through the air when the wind reached the peak of a gust and then dying away, sounding even more desolate as it faded.

'The weather's getting really bad,' said Sarah. She had almost no breath to speak as the air blustered into her face with increasing force. 'Maybe we should cut inland.'

'It's quicker to go straight along this way,' gasped Katie. The sign of Sea Spray Hotel, though tiny in the distance, was easy to see now she knew how to recognise it. 'But I bet the museum'll be shut.'

'Doesn't matter,' said Sarah. Then, 'At least it isn't raining.'

On an impulse, Katie linked arms with her and the

two of them battled on until, by mutual consent, they staggered across the road to the prom and ducked into one of the iron and glass Victorian shelters for a brief rest from all the buffeting. Even though they chose the inland side of the shelter, the wind still plucked at them through the open side. Still, the structure gave some protection and breathing was noticeably easier. So was talking.

'I'll tell you something,' said Sarah. 'I still feel bad for not telling him my mother's still alive.'

'It's simpler like this,' said Katie. 'You agreed.'

'Yes – but he has a right to know. She *was* his wife.'

Pent-up emotion and anger exploded out of Katie with a venom that surprised her. 'He has *no* rights,' she said. 'He wasn't fit to have a child. He had you *tortured* – for money . . .'

'Oh hey,' said Sarah, 'he wasn't *that* bad.'

'He was. He was vile. When you thought they'd used Christine when she was a child you said it was a terrible thing to do!'

'That's different.'

'How?'

'Because – I don't know – I think – you can't forgive someone for what they did to someone else, but you can forgive them for what they did to you.'

'That's mad! *And* he's not at all interested in you now. Or me. He didn't ask a single thing about us.'

'He asked where we live.'

'Oh, big deal! He didn't ask what the rest of your childhood was like, he didn't ask if you're happy, or what work you do, or if you're married, or what your life's like now. He just wanted to know if you remembered *him* and then he wanted to shove a stupid cheque at you to make himself feel better. He's only interested in himself and how he feels. He's selfish and . . . and . . . and *disgusting*!'

Sarah leant against the inside of the shelter, avoiding sitting on its graffiti-scarred seats. She scuffed aside a crisp wrapper that had rushed into the shelter after them, and the wind took it skittering away along the prom. 'You'd expected a monster,' she said. 'You weren't at all ready for what he really is – very ordinary – a bit weak, a bit greedy, a bit self-absorbed, a bit inclined to miss the point – very much like the rest of us.'

'You're not like him. You were *never* like him.'

'You don't know him. Neither of us knows him. If I hadn't had the accident I wouldn't have had the dream and then I don't suppose we'd ever have known what he did way back then.'

'But you *did* have the dream,' said Katie, 'and that proves the horrible, frightening memory was waiting there, in your head. *And* the accident was all his fault. You saw the ad for those horrible sweets he gave you and that's why you walked in front of the car. He's done *so much damage*!'

'You were the one who wanted to dig up the past. I'd have left it.'

The anger seeped rapidly away and Katie looked steadily at her mother while the wind battered against the side of the shelter and spilled in around its edges, spinning the dust and litter around their feet. 'Has it helped?' she said. 'Or have I made things worse?'

Sarah grabbed her and gave her a quick hug. 'Of course it's helped,' she said. 'I know what the dream is now, so I'll be able to let go of it. But you, Katie – you're going to have to let go of a lot of things too. Now let's get back before we get blown three towns down the coast.'

Even clinging together, to turn two light bodies into one heavier one, they were pushed about by the stronger gusts.

Not too far now to the hotel, and there was something cathartic and refreshing about walking, or staggering, along the promenade, right beside the beach, right beside the seething sea . . .

The tide was high and the heaving water, even at the shoreline, looked full and deep. If the wind had been blowing onshore the waves would have crashed right across the prom, but it was from the east so they ran sideways and could only claw fiercely at the bank of shingle and broken shells. Waves broke high under the distant pier and churned into white anger around the tops of the supports. Lines of whiteness on the crests of waves bit into the louring sky, right out to the horizon.

One arm firmly linked through her mother's, Katie put her free hand up to block first one ear then the other. The chill of the wind, and the terrible crying sound it made, was giving her earache.

As they passed the old lifeboat station, closed as they had expected, they both saw the figure at the same time – some way ahead, down on the shingle bank, alone, upright and slim. Christine – perilously close to the water's edge, swaying as each squall hit.

Though the wind direction meant the sea was

running on a slant, not beating directly at the shore, still the waves were bulky and powerful and every third or fourth one surged up and over her feet before it sank back again.

It struck Katie that she looked like a sacrificial offering – a gift to the sea – a gift it was horribly close to accepting.

She felt a sharp tug as Sarah pulled free and began to run. 'Christine!' she called. 'Be careful!' but the wind took her voice and shredded it and dispersed it amongst its own cries and howls.

Running after her, not shouting, just trying to keep up, Katie saw clearly the terrible, inevitable moment when the top of the unstable shingle bank gave way under Christine's feet.

There were no shallows here. The sea had spent months pilling up its own stony breakwater, and at the point where Christine was standing there was a drop of nearly seven feet to the level beach below; seven feet filled with grey-green water, its waves flexing like great muscles, their tops scudding towards the west.

As she slid she flung her arms out – for balance; then up – like a plea for mercy.

They were running, running, running – both shouting for help to an empty world – but it was over before they could reach her.

One moment she was sliding, stumbling, hands out, clutching at nothing – the next she was gone and the sea continued to swell and surge and the wind continued to howl and wail as though nothing of any importance had happened.

TWENTY-THREE

Easy to run along the flat surface of the prom, pushed on by the surging air currents from the east.

Not so easy to keep watching the exact spot where she'd slipped under the water, with the wind making their eyes sting and stream and blowing their hair across their faces.

The storm was so full of voices now – a roaring, and a howling, and that desperate, intermittent crying – that it seemed impossible anyone would hear their shouts for help.

Katie saw Sarah, just ahead of her, jump down on to the shingle bank. She followed, and they crunched and stumbled across the stones towards the place where the white wave-edges threatened.

And suddenly Christine was there – in the sea – her head above water and tipped back, her arms thrashing in panic, her hair a pale patch on the undulating surface of the dark water.

She was not far out, and for a moment it seemed it would be possible to reach her from the beach. Sarah dropped down on to her knees and stretched one arm out, as far as she could. Katie, tears streaming down her face, her ears full of the shrieking of the wind, knelt behind her, holding on to her other arm, to form a human rope.

But Christine had been washed too far offshore. In her floundering panic, she didn't see them, couldn't reach towards them – and sank again right in front of them.

Sarah shook herself free, twisted into a sitting position and dragged off her shoes. She was breathing rapidly, through her mouth, gasping for air – as though she was drowning in the wind.

'No!' Katie cried, dragging at her mother's arm to hold her back.

The running man passed them so suddenly that Katie screamed. The thousand voices of the wind and the greedy gulping sounds of the devouring waves had covered his approach.

He must have dragged off his boots as he ran and he was in the water beside the struggling girl within a second.

Even in the brief moment before he dived, the bulk of him and the glimpse of jeans, navy sweater, grey beard, was enough to identify John Craigie.

There was a long moment when the sea swallowed both Christine and her father.

Then he was surfacing again – and he had hold of her.

He clawed at the edge of the shingle bank with his free hand – and the sliding stones gave no support.

He clutched at Sarah's outstretched hand – but the waves broke over him and her fingers slipped through his.

All Katie could do was cling on to Sarah; terrified she would be pulled in and swallowed by the sea.

It was a moment of sound and horror that seemed to fill the universe.

But others had heard the shouts for help; others had run on to the beach. A young man flung himself flat on the stones beside Sarah, and together they managed to haul the big man and the half-drowned girl over the edge of the shingle ridge, where other hands could help to drag them ashore.

John Craigie and the young man struggled to their feet, but Christine, unable to stand, clung on to Sarah.

The other helpers stood back, assuming Sarah and Christine belonged together. The young man hurried away, beating damp shingle from his clothes as he went, to rejoin his girlfriend, who was standing on the promenade frozen with fear.

Christine leant forward and coughed out some sea water.

'Can you breathe?' said Sarah.

'Yes,' said Christine, her voice only a little hoarse. She coughed again and began to shiver.

Someone put a coat around her; someone else was calling an ambulance on his mobile.

There was an interval reverberating with relief and exhaustion. Katie felt the tears still running down her face. Christine was breathing all right now. Sarah's breathing was steadying.

Then Christine scraped her wet hair behind her ears and raised her head. Her face could only be described as radiant – so relaxed and happy she was almost unrecognisable.

'It's all right now,' she said in a clear voice. 'It's all over now.'

It seemed to Katie that she looked reborn. It was such a strange thought she half wondered if shock had affected her mind. Then a movement caught her eye and she looked round to see John Craigie, small in the distance, running towards them along the beach.

How odd that he'd left Christine so soon. Where had he gone? To fetch something? A rug to wrap her in? But no, he wasn't carrying anything.

The pounding of his boots along the shingle ridge drew closer. When had he had time to put his boots back on?

Then he was beside them, pulling Christine to her feet and hugging her and Katie noticed something else that was odd. His clothes were completely dry. Yet he couldn't possibly have changed in the few seconds he'd been missing.

'I heard her calling,' Christine was saying, 'then the beach gave way. It was so deep – I couldn't breathe . . . I'd have drowned if you hadn't pulled me out.'

'It wasn't me,' said John Craigie. He held her away from him, to look at her. 'You're all right? You're really all right?'

'It *was* you,' said Katie. 'I *saw* you.'

He ignored her. He could only look at Christine. 'I was clearing up in the museum,' he said. 'Someone banged on the door . . . said you were in the water – I thought I was going to lose you again . . .'

The ambulance pulled right on to the promenade. The paramedics hurried across the beach to the small knot of people and then led Christine and her father into it. The people who had run on to the beach dispersed, one woman carrying the damp coat she had draped around Christine.

Katie put her arms around Sarah and they hugged silently.

'John Craigie,' said Katie shakily. 'He said it wasn't him – I *saw* him.'

'I thought it was him,' said Sarah, 'but it can't have been. He came from way over there – and you could see he hadn't been in the water.'

'So who was it? And where did he go?'

Sarah looked at her steadily. 'John Craigie *does* look very like his father,' she said.

'But Bill Craigie died years ago,' said Katie. 'It can't have been him.'

Sarah didn't say anything.

'It *can't* have been,' said Katie. 'Can it?'

Sarah put her arm around her. 'It *is* quiet now,' she said, 'isn't it?'

In one way it was an odd thing to say – or shout – above the whistling of the wind, the surging of the sea and the grinding of the great waves mauling the top of the shingle bank – but in another way it was true.

The storm was fierce, and the creaking and rattling and groaning of the seafront buildings under siege from the gale formed a chorus that amplified the uproar – but the pitiful crying voice of a terrified drowning child had stopped, completely.

All the sounds made by the wind were just that – sounds made by the wind.

TWENTY-FOUR

The town didn't change outwardly. It was still tatty. Although today the sea that bordered it was dancing and sparkling in the sun, the surfaces of the buildings were still scarred and pitted by the erosive action of its damp and salty breath.

But the spirit of the town had changed. The waiting was over and the sense of oppression had lifted.

Past mistakes and failures – even unthinking, unintended torture – had been forgiven. And the needless self-torture of guilt that had haunted the dead as well as the living was dispersing and fading.

It was early in the day and only a few people were around near the promenade – a couple with a small dog, a man carrying a newspaper, a woman and a teenage girl.

The woman and the girl were cutting through the side streets to the nearest bus stop. The bags on their backs were full enough to suggest they were going to take the bus to the station. They had a happy, relaxed air about them. They were talking and laughing as they walked.

It seemed their visit to the town had been successful.

How does a story end? How does this one end?

Does it end suddenly, as the nightmares themselves

did? Does it end gradually – like the guilt and grief that faded and faded until no one heard the crying on the wind ever again?

Where does a story end? Where does this one end?

Does it go on to follow each of its characters in turn, to watch what happened to them next?

Does it go on to look at the local cinema in that seaside town, and to note that it, in common with other local cinemas all over the country, is currently showing a highly-acclaimed film in which a very small child – a boy this time – is required to scream in terror. Does it point out that he is far too young to be acting, as the tale of horror and destruction unfolds around him, and so his fear must be real? Does it follow him into later life to record the damage?

No. Every story has to stop somewhere – and, for this one, this is the place.